THE BOTTLE OF NEVER FORGETTING

THE MAGIC PEOPLE - BOOK 3

ANDI CUMBO-FLOYD

1

I wasn't with Jed when he found it. I'm glad I wasn't there, because I probably would have told him it was garbage, to just throw it away in a trashcan on our way home. I've never been a very curious person, and I don't like extra stuff lying around. So a little glass bottle, yeah, I probably would have told him to toss it.

I'm glad I wasn't there. Well, mostly I'm glad.

Jed and Charlie were riding their bikes at an abandoned house site down the road. The builder had started construction by digging a huge hole for the foundation, but he hadn't been back for months. Mr. Wilson said it was probably because they were waiting for permits or something, but I had the feeling they weren't coming back to finish the house. Either way, the big mounds of dirt they'd dug up made for great bike riding if you like the idea of careening down a red-clay hill and sliding to a stop inches before you dropped into a giant pit full of rainwater. I did not like this idea, but Jed and Charlie had spent almost every afternoon that spring over there. While his mom was away on business, Charlie had come to live with the

Wilsons again, resuming his place as Jed's older brother like they hadn't been apart for a few months.

Each day after school, they came in, ate four men's worth of snacks, and then peddled over to the pit. Jed usually grunted a "hello" to me, his oldest friend, in passing, and Charlie always gave a polite nod of his head. But they didn't have time for a woman in her sixties, not just then, not even though I'd been Jed's best friend since he was born. As his imaginary and then not-so-imaginary friend, I'd grown to accept, if not love, that my role in his life would be different with each passing year. He didn't need me to keep him company during thunderstorms anymore, but he still liked having me around. I could tell because he always winked at me and smiled. It's amazing what a little wink and a grin can do for a woman's heart.

Whenever Jed and Charlie came home for dinner, Mrs. Wilson always had a basin of water and clean towels at the side door of the farmhouse, and she made them wash up and strip down to their boxers before walking across her clean floors. The boys grumbled the whole time, but they did it, sprinting through the house in their underwear while their mom and I averted our eyes. Then, we all ate dinner before the boys did their homework. We were a family, a hodgepodge one that wasn't entirely biological or legally connected, but a family nonetheless.

Most days, I was content to spend my time reading books, watching TV, and hanging out with our friends who lived on the farm now—Alonso and Lakeemba and especially Sharon. I loved her no-holds-barred attitude and wished I had more of that. Maybe then I wouldn't miss Jed so much. I appreciated that he didn't need me, sure, but I still missed him. In fact, I missed when I was imaginary—when only Jed could see me— and when he trusted me with everything.

Mostly, though, I was content with the quiet life. I'd tried to get a job, or I'd started to try to get a job, but Mrs. Wilson had pointed out that I didn't really have the right documentation—like a birth certificate or social security number—that would make that possible, so I worked hard to earn my keep by helping out around the house and farm. I'd even learned to fold a fitted sheet so that it didn't look like a balled-up pile of fabric. The Wilsons had made it clear: I didn't have to do work, but it made me feel better to not just be a burden.

Still, I missed carrying my weight by being Jed's confidant. I missed talking with him. My favorite days were still when he went to bed, and he let me sit beside him, rubbing his back until he fell asleep. Sometimes, when he was feeling particularly calm, he'd tell me about his day.

The day he found the bottle was one of those days. He'd been especially quiet since coming back from the pit that evening, and I'd kept an eye on him as he did his algebra homework. He was particularly frustrated that night. Algebra was always hard for Jed. The rules just didn't click with him, and he hated it. But he kept going, determined to figure it out, every night. That night, though, he kept breaking the tips off his pencil and swearing under his breath. High school had given him a whole new vocabulary, and sometimes I had to look up the words he used when he was upset. The imaginary friend operating system hadn't come equipped with swear words.

Finally, he threw down his pencil and stormed off to his room. Charlie looked at me and shrugged. Mrs. Wilson started to follow him, putting down her cross-stitch and standing up, but when she saw me, she nodded. We'd come to an understanding, Jed's parents and I. Sometimes, having a grandma-age formerly-imaginary friend was helpful, and tonight, I got to help.

I followed Jed to his room and knocked at the door. "Go away," he said.

"If you really want me to, I will," I answered, "but if you want to tell me what's going on, I'm here." I waited a minute, and when he didn't answer, I slid down the wall and sat beside the door. "I'll just wait then."

I could hear Jed's bed creaking as he shifted around, and then, one of his desk drawers opened. Those sounds I would recognize anywhere; I'd heard them so often over the past fifteen years.

Finally, I knocked again, very quietly, "Jed, can I come in?"

He made a sound that I decided to interpret as a grunt of permission and went in. He was sitting on his bed, long legs hanging over the side to the floor, and he had a small brown bottle in his hands. The bottle looked like one of those old medicine bottles you see at antique shops and flea markets. It was made of glass, and the top was covered in wax, like someone had dripped an old, red candle over the cork.

I sat down and let my legs sway off the bed next to him. "What's that?"

He looked up at me like he was surprised I was this close and then turned his gaze back to the bottle. "I found it today, over by the pit."

"Oh. Maybe someone tossed it there. I pick up a lot of trash on my walks. People are ridiculous with their litter."

He shook his head. "It's not litter . . . or not litter from now."

I felt the skin on the back of my neck tingle. "What do you mean?" I looked more closely at the bottle and could see what looked like scratches all over it.

"It's old, and it's carrying something inside it. I can see it."

That tingly feeling got stronger. Jed had always been able to see things people couldn't, so if he was seeing something now, then something was there. "What do you see?" I kept my voice quiet, casual. Too much interest on my part and he'd clam up.

"These are words." He laid his pointer finger on some of the scratches. "I can't read them, but I almost can. They're a warning, I think."

I let out a long sigh. "If they're a warning, maybe you'd

better put it back, Jed." We've had enough danger in the past two years to fill a lifetime, and I wasn't keen to find more.

He looked at me then, his eyes sad. "You know I can't, Mavis."

My heart ached. He looked so tired, and at fifteen, a boy should be tired because he's worried about the person he likes or a test, not because he needed to help save people, again. "Jed, maybe LaKeemba and Alonso and them can take it. Maybe they can handle it." We had friends, magical friends, who would help. And since they lived right here, having moved in the hayfield in a cluster of yurts after one of our adventures a couple years back, it wouldn't even be hard to ask for their help. I clenched my jaw in the hopes that he'd let me take it to LaKeemba and be done with it.

His eyes turned back to the bottle. "You know I can't just give this over, Mavis. That's not how it works."

I sighed. I did know. Gifts like Jed's—gifts like mine—came with responsibility. Our friends, the magic people, had taught us both that, and while gifts were wonderful in stories, in life, they were often quite heavy. This tiny brown bottle felt heavy. So heavy already.

"Okay. But tonight, let's put it away. Keep it close by but separate. We can't figure it out tonight. Tomorrow, we'll go see LaKeemba."

Jed nodded, and when I put out my hand, he set the bottle in it.

I stood and placed the bottle on the top of his dresser, next to approximately one million pairs of socks that had not made the trip one inch down to his drawer.

"Right after breakfast, Mavis, okay?"

Tomorrow was a school day, but both Jed and I knew his parents would let him stay home for this. They were good like that. They understood what Jed could do, and they made space for it. If anything, that was the most beautiful part of all these adventures, watching them come to understand and to accept. It wasn't always like that in families. Charlie's family of origin was evidence of that.

THE NEXT MORNING, Jed carried the bottle with him to breakfast and set it on the table. As Mrs. Wilson slid scrambled eggs and orange slices onto Jed's plate, he explained about finding the bottle and needing to talk to LaKeemba. "It's not just an old bottle, Mom."

Charlie was not one to miss an adventure, so he added, "See those markings. They mean something, don't you think?"

Mr. Wilson came in from feeding the chickens then and sat down. "What means something?" he asked before taking a long sip of his coffee.

"They look like words, or sentences, or something. They're not just random scratches from being buried or whatever," Jed added.

The bottle was small, shorter than my pointer finger, and thin. It looked like it could only hold one dose of something. I picked it up and turned it around and around, studying the markings. "They do look intentional," I said and passed it over to Mrs. Wilson as she took her seat.

As the bottle made its way around the table, we all ate, slowly and quietly, like we were waiting. Maybe we were. The past couple years' adventures had taught us all about patience, about when to hurry and when to pause.

Finally, the bottle passed back to Jed, and he said, "So can I stay home and go out to the see LaKeemba today?"

"Me, too?" Charlie added. He had never taken to school after traveling into our time, even though he did well. It just wasn't what he thought he'd be doing when he was eighteen. At his first home, he would have already been helping his father run the plantation. Now, he was in a classroom doing science experiments and giving reports on the years he lived through as though they'd happened long ago, which they had, but not for him. So any chance he got to stay at his new home on the Wilsons' farm, he took.

Mr. and Mrs. Wilson looked at each other, and I knew then that they'd decided. The boys would be staying home today, and I felt a thrill of excitement and trepidation pass up my spine. I liked when they were home.

A new adventure—I was eager and terrified, so pretty normal for our escapades.

"We'll all go over and see her after breakfast," Mr. Wilson said. He tried to look stern and serious, but I could see the smile at the corner of his mouth. He was ready for a new adventure. I hoped we all were.

2

———

When we first met the magic people, they'd lived near the farm, just in another time period, Charlie's time, back in the 1800s. That first trip through time had been a doozy, and it had resulted in them needing a new place—a new time really—to live in. So the Wilsons let them set up that small gathering of yurts at the top of the hayfield.

The Wilsons had built a yurt for me, too. Mine was a bit closer to the farmhouse, but we all lived pretty near one another, near enough to see each other in passing most days. I thought of it as our magical commune, and it was like a dream come true for me, all these people I loved right here, nearby. I'd spent so much of my life invisible to everyone except for Jed. And now that I was visible—unless I didn't want to be—I loved the chance to casually chat with people as we trimmed the goat's hooves or walked up and down the farm lane with armloads of vegetables for the farm stand that Sharon now ran for the Wilsons. It felt like we lived in town but without all the traffic.

LaKeemba was the de facto leader of the magic people. A

tall, thin woman with walnut-brown skin and long dreadlocks, she had the sort of presence that made you feel both immediately at ease and also like you wanted to impress her somehow but knew you couldn't. I liked her a lot, and more, I respected her, trusted her. I had to. She'd saved my life more than once.

But it was Sharon, the healer, who had become my dearest friend, next to Jed, of course. She didn't hold back when she had something to say, and while I didn't always want to hear the truth—who does?—I was always glad I'd listened. I spent a lot of my days up in the farm stand with her. I'd help her with bagging up vegetables for people who stopped by and organizing the Little Free Library that we'd started up there, too.

This morning, they must have been expecting us—not surprising since everyone who had magic, except me for whatever reason—had a kind of telepathy. It wasn't really like they were reading one another's thoughts but more like they worked as hive, anticipating and coordinating with the others.

As the five of us walked up the small hill from the farmhouse to the yurts, LaKeemba came out of her round tent and raised a hand in greeting. "Good to see you," she said. "I wondered if you would all come." She put a hand on Charlie's head, tousling his red hair, and smiled. "I'm glad you're here."

Charlie's arrival in our time hadn't been simple, and for a long time, he'd been a little bristly around LaKeemba because, I guess, he blamed her for what had happened. Probably easier to blame her than your own daddy. Now, though, he seemed to have let his guard down, and I noticed that LaKeemba always made a little special effort to make him feel at home.

"Please come in," she said and stepped aside from the door. Her yurt was always filled with the best smells, like the beach and a campfire and cinnamon all wrapped into one. The walls were covered with bright fabrics, lots of purple and red, and to one side of the single room, she'd set up a circle of cushions so guests could sit together and talk. The first few times I'd visited her, she'd offered to find me a chair—I wasn't the epitome of grace when it came to sitting on the floor, but all the work on the farm had made me stronger—so I slid down to the rug, not easily, but without a groan this time.

Sharon came in while LaKeemba was getting us tea, and my friend sat down beside me and took my pale hand in her light-brown one. "Sounds like big news?"

I shrugged. "Not sure. But maybe." I squeezed her hand. She had a way of making me feel safe, secure.

Jed, on my other side, was fidgety, all bouncing knees and cracking knuckles. I understood. Like him, I was one of those people who liked to get things over with, even if it meant having to deal with some hard stuff. The waiting was the worst part.

Still, we knew that LaKeemba would take the time she took. She was not a woman to be hurried, which was probably why we trusted her. She gathered information and sat with it a long while before she acted. I admired that . . . but it made me anxious, too.

Eventually, LaKeemba sat down and put out her hand to Jed. He placed the bottle in her palm, and as he did, I noticed for the first time that it kind of glowed. It wasn't bright like a light bulb but more like one of those glow-in-the-dark stickers that needed a recharge.

She studied the bottle and ran her fingers over the scratches in the glass. Then, she passed it Sharon, who did the same. The two women exchanged a glance, and Sharon said, "I'll go get him." My friend lithely stood from her cushion and went out of the door.

"We need Alonso for this conversation," LaKeemba explained. "Meanwhile, could you tell me where you found this, Jed and Charlie?"

Jed looked over at Charlie, and I saw the kindness in his eyes. He so badly wanted to claim this bottle as his own, but he knew Charlie needed to be a part of this. "You tell them, Charlie."

A small smile passed over Charlie's lips before he began to describe the construction site and the pile of dirt. "The top was just sticking up, and we thought it might just be some trash." He looked at Mrs. Wilson, who smiled. "We try to pick up trash whenever we see it. But once we dug it out, it didn't look like trash at all."

Jed let him finish before he added, "It's carrying something." He stared at the bottle on the floor in the middle of our circle. "But I can't see what. It's like it's hiding from me."

LaKeemba nodded. "I think you may be right, Jed. Someone has taken time to obscure what is inside."

The door of the yurt opened, and a large black man entered with Sharon. I couldn't help but smile. Alonso was special. His magic was that he could touch someone and ease their discomfort, and while I enjoyed that I could become invisible at will—especially when sneaking up on Jed—I thought that if I could have my choice of powers, it would be Alonso's. Giving comfort seemed like a special kind of magic.

But then, I kind of thought that Alonso was maybe magical in general. I hadn't told him that, though. I didn't know how. He gave me a wide smile before he folded himself down on the cushion beside Mr. Wilson. Then, he reached over, picked up the bottle, and said, "Memory."

I waited for more information, to hear about the memory that Alonso was talking about. But as the silence grew longer, I wondered if he'd seen a bottle like this before, or maybe even this bottle. That would be weird, but weirder things have happened. Yet, when he started to speak, the story wasn't about him at all.

"You all know the stories about the genies in the bottles. You rub them and get three wishes," Alonso began. Alonso's voice had taken on a gentle rocking sound, a lilt I think you'd call it, and I felt myself settle into my bones a bit more, ready for the story.

"Well, this bottle is like those, but it doesn't hold a genie. In here, is the central thread of memory."

He paused, and I was, as always, about to ask questions when he spoke again.

"Many years ago, more years than any of us can remember, a magical person bound the center of memory into this bottle. Then, they etched a warning about opening the bottle into the side. I expect they thought everyone would be able to read it because everyone could read magic-speak then, even a little. But most of us have lost the gift."

I couldn't help myself. "You can read it though?"

Alonso's soft eyes met mine. "I can. It says, 'Be wary. Herein rest all the memories of the world. Open at your peril.'" He set the bottle back in the middle of the circle and let out a long sigh. "I've heard tale of this bottle, of the way that it looses memories forgotten but also those hidden out of peril. We must be wise here."

Mrs. Wilson cleared her throat. "Am I understanding this right? If we open it, every memory will return to every person in the world? No one will be able to forget anything?"

"That's right. But not only will they not forget in the future, but they will also remember everything they've ever known or experienced," Alonso's voice was solemn.

Next to me, Jed stirred, "Remembering is good, right? Our history teacher Mr. Muir is always quoting something about being doomed to repeat history if we forget it. He says that if we don't remember what happened with things like Wounded Knee or the Holocaust, it becomes too easy for them to happen again." His voice was high with excitement, "So if we let this out, then no one will be able to forget again, right?"

"True enough, Jed," Sharon said, "But it's not that simple. Some things need forgetting."

Mr. Wilson furrowed his brow. "I don't know about that. I believe in the truth, in how the truth will set us free."

Jed nodded and opened his mouth to speak, but it was Charlie's voice that entered the circle. "I don't think I will survive if I remember everything."

A wide-open silence of pain entered the tent then as we thought about Charlie's father, about his hatefulness, about how he'd cast out his own son just because he was magical. I didn't know all of Charlie's story; I didn't think anyone did, maybe not even he did. I could see what he meant.

We sat in that quiet a long time, and I weighed the truth of history against the truth of pain. I kept coming back to the good of the many versus the good of the few, and I couldn't find my way through that question, not with Charlie right there. The good of the many just couldn't be more important than my friend. It couldn't be more important than someone I loved and saving him from memory that might kill him. Could it?

After a while, Alonso spoke again. "Maybe we need to consider why the bottle is here, now."

Jed was a smart kid, but sometimes, he was a little literal. "It's here because I dug it up, and I dug it up because they dug that big hole for that house up the road." He sounded grumpy, like he was a toddler again and one who needed a snack.

"True, Jed. But there hasn't always been a pit for a foundation just up the road, right? And you have ridden there many days and never found this, right?" LaKeemba's voice was firm but gentle. "You two found the bottle, and if someone else had, they likely would have thrown it away or maybe kept it as an antique. They wouldn't have known it held something. Only you could see that." She gave Jed a long look. "There are too many coincidences—the when and the where and the who—for this to be happenstance."

I looked over at Jed, and he was blushing. I couldn't tell if it was from embarrassment or pride.

"Someone wanted us to find it?" I asked.

LaKeemba nodded. "I think so."

A flash of insight passed through my mind. "Someone who walks time, too." I felt a chill of fear and exhilaration pass through me. Someone had come into our time and left the bottle for Jed and Charlie specifically. I could spend a long time trying to puzzle out whether that person had been from the future or the past, but really, the when didn't matter. As always, what mattered was what we were being asked to do right now.

Mr. Wilson let out a long stream of air through his pursed lips. "Then, I guess we need to decide what to do."

"Open it or don't open it?" his wife added.

"I vote 'don't,'" Charlie said quickly, and when I looked at him, I saw the terror in his eyes. Mrs. Wilson must have seen it too because she scooted closer to him and put her hand on his back.

"I'm with Charlie. I mean, I want to prevent horrible things, like Mr. Muir said, but this seems like too much, too much all at once. I have a bad feeling," Jed added.

Mrs. Wilson's voice was very soft when she spoke, and her eyes were sad when she looked at Jed and Charlie. Still, she didn't hesitate. "I think we should open it." It felt like the air vibrated around her words, a little like they were a bit pointy, shaped to reach deep into the ear of the one who heard them. "We were given this gift—or maybe this curse—for a reason. I don't know how we can see the reason until we know what happens when we open the bottle."

I tensed up, and Charlie set his jaw. Jed looked from his mom to his foster brother and back again.

"We can't know the result of opening it either," Mr. Wilson's voice was dark. "I vote no." I saw him give his wife a sad look, and I sighed. I hated when people disagreed. I especially hated when people I loved disagreed.

A long silence stretched out into the room, and I was just

about to voice my argument for why we shouldn't open it when Alonso saved us from a debate. "This is not, in my opinion, something we debate. This is something we come to a consensus on. Either we all agree, or we do nothing."

"Yes, we cannot take this to a vote like we're choosing what to have on our pizza," Sharon added. "We talk it out and think about it until we all know."

Jed groaned. "That could take forever."

"It could, but big choices are worth holding, Jedidiah." Sharon's voice was low and firm. "We held the one about whether to trust you, and it was a good choice. It wouldn't have been if we'd forced some of us to go along."

That flush of color went up Jed's face, and I knew it was embarrassment this time.

"Time is of the essence, though, so we will meet back here later today to talk again," LaKeemba's tone signaled our gathering was over, so we all stood and made our way into the spring sunshine. I didn't know why, but sunshine always helped.

I SPENT the rest of the day outside. The flower beds around the farm needed to be weeded, and I loved weeding. It was so simple, kept my body moving, and gave me a sense of accomplishment. Nothing says, "I've done something," like a clean flower bed and a huge pile of weeds to feed the chickens. When Mrs. Wilson had first told me that, I'd been skeptical, but she was right.

Plus, weeding was good for thinking, and I needed to think. As I began tugging out the clover and grass from around the big stump that Mrs. Wilson had turned into a planter and the flower bed, I tried to remember everything I'd ever known like Alonso said I would if the bottle were opened. I pushed hard into those first days with Jed when I'd appeared here on the farm. He was tiny then, just back from the hospital, and he couldn't even see me. I tried to sit with him because I knew that's what I was supposed to do, but it was so boring and so exhausting since he never slept. I had been really lonely, lonely and worried. I thought maybe I hadn't been doing my job right.

In time, it had gotten easier, but still, there had been a lot of sad days—days when the Wilsons went on vacations, and I couldn't go. Days when they were caught up in something as a family and Jed didn't even glance my way. Days when I wished with all my heart that someone would just see me and talk to me, someone besides a kid who mostly wanted me to play with cars and read him books. Just remembering those days was painful, even though everything got better for me, something I'd realized would happen even back in those hard days.

But then I thought of Sharon's life as a little girl. She'd been a slave at Charlie's dad's plantation. Mostly she didn't talk about it, but when she did, she told tales of having to fetch water for the house from the stream. She had carried bucket after bucket of water up the hill all day long. I'd asked her once how old she'd been when she started working. "I don't rightly know, Mavis. Maybe six. Seven." A seven-year-old girl doing hard labor all day. Would Sharon want to remember that all the way? Were there harder things she'd lived through that she did not remember? Did she want to?

As I made my way to weed around the marigolds by the barn, I thought about what Jed's history teacher had said. I wondered if remembering could keep another little girl from going through what Sharon had gone through. Would it keep another little boy from being hated by his father as Charlie had been? Would it keep slavery from happening again?

I wasn't getting much of anywhere in my thinking, but I'd already pulled enough weeds to feed the chickens for two days. So I loaded up the wheelbarrow and took the birds their treats —they loved to scratch at a pile of weeds to find their favorite kinds, and I loved to watch. After dumping the wheelbarrow, I went into the farmhouse and got a glass of ice water before sitting on the Wilsons' deck and staring across the farmyard. My thinking hadn't gotten me closer to an answer. So maybe not thinking would.

The birds had spread the weeds out like a carpet in the pen when I heard Jed and Charlie talking from the other side of the coop. They'd been out in the goat pasture checking fence-line, a chore they'd both grumbled about when Mr. Wilson assigned it this morning but one that I knew they kind of enjoyed, too. Those boys needed to move around. If they sat still too long, playing video games and such, they got grumpy, and having two grumpy teenagers around is brutal. It was like being trapped in a house with two giraffes who whined a lot and never liked what there was to eat.

Plus, checking fence lines meant they got to play with the baby goats, and all of us liked to play with those kids. They bounced around like they had springs for legs, and they butted your legs to try and knock you down so they could jump on you. Ask me how I know.

The boys didn't sound particularly playful today as they came up the last stretch of fence behind the chicken coop. "I know, Charlie. It would be hard for you to remember all of that, but could it help to remember, too?"

Charlie's sigh was so loud I could hear it all the way around the small building between us. "I don't know. Maybe. But Jed, I think there's a reason I can't remember things. Maybe they're too hard or something; maybe my brain is protecting me, like putting up a force field so I don't fall apart in remembering."

There was a silence, and then I heard the fence puller ratcheting the welded wire tight again as Jed grunted under the effort. "Okay, like repression, right? Did they talk about that in your history class?"

There was another grunt, this time from Charlie. He must

have been attaching the fence holders to the posts. "No," he said. "Mr. Greer doesn't talk about anything but the Vietnam War."

"Oh, right," Jed answered, and I pictured the thin, wild-haired teacher who ran the school's theater program and showed war movies instead of teaching most days. "Well, repression is when your mind hides things from you, painful things that might be too hard for you to handle. Mr. Muir calls it a trauma response. It's your mind's way of protecting you."

Their voices came a few steps closer. "Well, maybe that's what's happened to me. I don't remember many things, or if I remember, the details are unclear, as if I dreamed them," Charlie said.

"Have you tried to remember?" Jed's voice was soft, easy, but still, that was a big question. I sat forward in my chair, ready to go to them if this was too much for Charlie.

I heard a soft thud in the grass, and then Charlie said, "Kind of, but not really. If my mind is protecting me, maybe I shouldn't."

"Maybe. Or maybe it's better to remember on your own terms, when you want to. Especially if..." His voice trailed off.

"Especially if we decide to open the bottle." A long pause stretched out across the farmyard. "Okay." Charlie's voice was quiet, and then I heard him take a deep breath.

JEDIDIAH

I felt pretty terrible for asking Charlie to remember. I didn't know all that happened to him back then, but I knew it sucked. But I also knew Charlie, and he was a good person. If opening the bottle could help, he'd want us to open it. I hoped that maybe remembering something now would be easier than remembering it all later.

What I didn't think about was how awful it would be for me to hear what he remembered, and it was so awful. He told me about this time when he was very little, maybe four or five, he thought, and he'd stopped time for fun, making all the chickens in the plantation yard stand still.

"I was not yet in full control of my magic, so I only could pause pockets of time. I enjoyed that, though, because I liked to see the chickens frozen in front of me while the rest of the world kept moving." He had his eyes closed as he told me, and it seemed like when he remembered one thing, more came back to him.

"Someone must have seen me, though, because the next thing I knew, Daddy's hand was on the back of my neck. He picked me up by my hair and told me to stop my foolishness. I released the chickens, but he didn't let go of me." Charlie's voice was thick, but I didn't look

at him. I didn't like for people to watch me when I cried, and I didn't think he'd like it either.

"He carried me to the stocks, put a block of wood under my feet so my head and arms would reach, and locked me in."

"Stocks? Like the ones we saw at Williamsburg last year?" I remembered the big blocks of wood into which prisoners who were being punished were placed. A family had put their little girl's head in them while we read the plaque nearby. They had holes for the person's head and arms, and they locked shut so they couldn't move. When we'd seen them, Charlie had shuddered. Mom had seen his expression and suggested to the girls' parents that maybe they weren't such good toys. They hadn't listened and kept laughing as Mom got more and more frantic and began to cry. We walked away.

"Yes, like those." His voice was very quiet now. "He left me there for the rest of the day. I got a terrible sunburn, and when the overseer finally came with the key about dark, I couldn't even stand up all the way." I pictured a little boy all crooked from being bent forward for hours, and this time, I shuddered.

"That is horrible. I can't believe he'd do that to anyone, especially his kid," I was trying to keep from crying, but when I got mighty angry, I cried. Mavis said that was a good thing, that it gave me a way to let it all out. But I didn't want to make what had happened to Charlie about me.

"Father did it often. That day, one of our slaves was in the stocks next to me. He'd been ten minutes late getting back from visiting his wife at the Beazley place down the road. Father left him in the stocks for two days without food." He stood up and moved back to the fence we were re-stretching.

We worked for a while in silence, and then Charlie said, quietly, "I will remember, Jed. But I will need help carrying all that."

"I've got you," I said as I gave the fence stretcher another tug. "I've got you."

3

———

That afternoon when the boys came around the coop after finishing their fence work, they dropped onto the steps up to the deck. I moved over to sit with them and plopped down next to Charlie, close enough to put my shoulder against him, and Jed did the same on his other side. I'd told them about hearing them talking, because I didn't want them to think I was eavesdropping, although I guess I kind of was, but also because I wanted Charlie to know I was here for him, too. He had nodded when I said he wasn't alone, but he wouldn't look at me. I couldn't imagine how hard this would be, but I admired his courage for stepping back in. And I worried what stepping back into his memories might do to him.

A bit later, when all the chores were done, Jed, Charlie, Mr. and Mrs. Wilson, and I headed up to the circle of yurts in the hayfield, and I saw Sharon stirring a big pot of stew over the fire in the middle of the gathering. All the buildings had electricity, and there were bathrooms, too, but sometimes, especially for celebrations or big conversations, we all preferred to gather around a fire and talk. It felt special then, those times together, in the way only open air and the dance of flames could make it feel.

The air was cooling, but the fire was quite warm. Mrs. Wilson had brought up blankets, and she and Mr. Wilson distributed them to the folks who needed them. Then, we grabbed bowls, got some of Sharon's stew, and sat down.

LaKeemba spoke. "I believe," she looked softly at Charlie and then at Jed, "that we have reached consensus."

Charlie nodded. "We can open the bottle," he said with a soft, clear voice.

Jed looked frustrated, like he was being forced to do something he didn't want to do, but he nodded, too. He wasn't going to stand against Charlie, not after what Charlie had told him. I put my arm around his shoulder and gave him a quick squeeze.

Sharon moved to sit next to Charlie. "I'll be here the whole time, Charlie. I'll heal you up quick if you need it." She gave his shoulder a quick pat, and he sighed. I hadn't really thought about how Sharon's healing powers might work on trauma, but now, it seemed only right. After all, mental illness was just illness, same as anything else. I'd have to think about why I hadn't realized that before.

We all sat quietly for a moment, the fire warming us as we let the chill of the spring day reach our backs. My mind was split. I definitely thought we needed to open the bottle, and I was eager, like fire, to get it over with, but when I looked at Charlie, a chill of worry ran up my spine. I hoped he would be okay. He was a strong kid, but that was because he'd had to be strong in a way that I never had. I hoped he could take it when all the details of his life came rushing back, and I was glad Sharon was going to help.

After a few minutes, Beatrice came out of her yurt; her body bent into a semi-circle toward her cane. It had been a long time since I'd seen my friend. She kept to herself mostly, enjoying hours of streaming TV and knitting baby blankets for the local hospital. Sharon had told me that Beatrice found the stories fascinating because they were illusions, just like the ones she could cast, but they didn't make her tired the same way. "When you're 104, you get to watch all the TV you want," Sharon had added, and I'd wholeheartedly agreed. If I lived that long, I was going to eat cake, pound caramel popcorn, and binge Netflix from dawn to dusk.

Now, the illusionist was sitting down in a lawn chair next to LaKeemba, and Alonso moved over next to her. "Beatrice is going to contain the memories in here, with those of us sitting around the fire, for a time," LaKeemba said. "We need to see what we are dealing with before we let it go."

LaKeemba looked at Alonso, who put his hand on Beatrice's arm. The older woman gave a slight nod and then turned her hands so her palms were facing the sky. She closed her eyes, and then she nodded once.

"Jed, since you found the bottle, you should open it." LaKeemba looked at him.

I turned to face my friend. All the color had drained from his face, and his hands were shaking. But he already had the bottle in front of him, his index finger fingernail under the seal of wax at the top.

"Ready?" he said with a glance around the circle. Everyone nodded, and he popped the seal.

I don't know what I'd expected—a thread of magic to spin out of the top or maybe a genie like that woman from the old TV show who could fold her arms and grant a wish. Instead, I couldn't see anything, and for the briefest of moments, I felt relief, but then a wash of disappointment moved up my torso.

I remembered the day Jed came home from the hospital with his parents. He was tiny, so small that, in the car seat, he looked like a baby doll. Mrs. Wilson had needed an emergency C-section to deliver him after almost forty hours of labor, and she walked like every step hurt. Mr. Wilson didn't look much better, deep circles under his eyes and worry in the corners of his mouth.

The first hours home were hard—Jed wasn't nursing well, and Mrs. Wilson was almost too tired to stay awake and feed him. Mr. Wilson did his best to help, but there wasn't much he could do besides get her glasses of water, hold the baby when she was sleeping, and vacuum the rug in their bedroom again and again.

Jed wouldn't sleep that night at all. He just cried and cried. Mrs. Wilson would try to feed him, but the baby couldn't get the right grip to eat. So he'd fall asleep but then wake up crying as soon as they laid him in his bassinet.

Finally about three a.m., Mr. Wilson found a sample bottle of formula in a bag of things a store had given them when they set up their gift registry. He put a tiny nipple on the bottle and put it to Jed's mouth, and that baby gulped down the food.

As he ate, Mrs. Wilson sobbed. "They told us not to give him formula. They said I needed to figure out how to nurse. He was starving."

As soon as Jed finished that first bottle, he slept hard, and the Wilsons collapsed into their own bed, exhausted by sleep-deprivation and worry. I had stayed up all night, keeping watch on them all as they went through the cycle of feeding and sleeping until Mr. Wilson got up to go to the store and buy more formula. It was the most beautiful and most terrifying night of my life.

And I relived it right there by that fire in the blink of an eye. I tried to hold back the waves of memory—every moment with Jed and his family, every journey with our magical friends, every French fry I'd ever eaten—but it was all there, parading through my mind like I was watching a movie of my own life.

I looked at the people around me, and they were silent and still. I presume because their memories were moving swift and fast around them. Charlie grimaced, and Sharon held on tighter, her eyes wide. Beatrice's hands rested quiet on her lap with her palms upturned, but I could see the strain of her effort on her face, even as Alonso did the double work of strengthening her and managing his memories. Mr. and Mrs. Wilson looked dumbstruck. Mrs. Wilson's mouth was hanging open, and Mr. Wilson squinted into the distance like he was watching something very far away. Only LaKeemba looked peaceful for the most part, but I could see her jaw clench.

Jed, though, Jed looked outright stricken. He stared straight ahead, and his mouth hung open.

I reached over and touched his arm, and he started like I'd snuck up on him.

LaKeemba looked over at the movement, and when she saw Jed's face—all drawn and pale—she spoke, "Memories, friends. These are memories. They cannot hurt us. They cannot help us, either."

Finally, Jed blinked, and he turned to me. "Mavis, what have we done?"

4

———————

I looked down at the bottle in Jed's hands and hoped I'd see that I could, somehow, reseal it. But the wax was broken, and the cork that had been below that had crumbled. What was done was done.

I looked out beyond our circle around the fire and saw the other magic people moving around with the end of the day activities. Lizzie was helping Marcus guide the chickens toward their coop, and Elwood was walking in from the vegetable garden, a basket full of lettuce in his hand. Beatrice's vision was holding around us, but I knew she couldn't keep it up forever. I knew we couldn't sit here forever either.

Another glance around our circle and I saw a smile flicker across Mrs. Wilson's face, and Sharon sighed as though she'd just eaten the best ice cream she'd ever had. I focused back on my memories and saw Jed as a little boy. He'd just gotten his first bicycle, and he was making his dad take off the training wheels. The little red bike was built for a preschooler, but Jed rode it like he was ready to race Lance Armstrong. I felt tears prick my eyes. Jed had been so happy, and so I had been happy too.

I looked back at Jed and saw that he had some color in his cheeks again. A wave of relief washed over me, and I laughed, hard. Something about all these memories, good and bad, made me a little hysterical, and the more I laughed, the harder it was to stop laughing. Soon, I was doubled over and trying not to pee as I rocked back and forth by the fire.

My laughter broke people's attention away from their memories, I guess, because soon Sharon was laughing, too, and then Mr. Wilson. Eventually, everyone in the circle, even Beatrice, had tears streaming down their faces as we all laughed like we'd just heard the best joke ever.

Jed even got going, too, and eventually, he said, "This isn't funny, you know?" while he tried to keep from laughing more. And we all cracked up further.

It took a few more minutes for us all to get our breath back, and by then, the memories—mine at least—had moved back a little. They weren't so in my face.

Sharon looked at me, "Thank you, Mavis. I needed that."

I blushed. "I didn't do it on purpose, but thanks."

"I suspect that's the reason it worked, Mavis. Your laughter was genuine and true. And it was of now, not then," LaKeemba said. "We needed to be brought back, pulled into this place and time. Laughter did that."

I thought of the yoga classes that I sometimes went to with Mrs. Wilson, about how the teacher told us to let our thoughts float by like clouds so that we didn't try to fix things or plan for what we were doing next. I couldn't do the cloud thing for long, but even trying to do it made me relax. Maybe that's what laughing had done just now.

Charlie stood up and gave his arms and legs a good shake. He hadn't laughed as hard as we did, but I knew that was because he just wasn't that kind of person. He kept a lot inside because he'd learned he had to. Now, though, he was smiling, and I thought he looked relieved. He'd survived.

He turned to Beatrice. She'd closed her eyes, and I could see her shoulders beginning to fold forward. "Want me to stop time around us for a minute? Give Beatrice a break while we choose what's next?" he asked LaKeemba.

"That's an excellent plan, Charlie. Please." LaKeemba waved her hand around the circle as she stood and stretched her hands above her head.

Charlie reached his own hand out in front of him, his palm facing Alonso across the circle. I looked over at the chicken coop and saw Lizzie's foot in mid-air, sole out, as she fended off the charging rooster. Time was stopped.

I knew Charlie couldn't hold it for long, so we needed to act fast. "There's no going back now," I said.

Jed looked down at the bottle. "No, there's not. So what do we do?"

Alonso stood and helped Beatrice to her feet. The woman spoke; her voice quiet but clear as a bell. "Now, we wait."

I almost groaned at her words, hated them something fierce. I was so much better with something to do.

Sharon reached her hands over her head in a tall stretch, "Wait for what? Probably not gonna be too good if *we* need to be doing something about it."

I did groan this time because I knew she was right. I wasn't sure who pulled the strings of the universe—God maybe—but whoever it was had seen fit to get this bottle to Jed and Charlie and then to the rest of us for some reason. I was willing to bet that reason wasn't going to be something fun.

"Let's get waiting then," Jed said, and I started to giggle again. Jed hated inaction even more than I did, so it was perfect that he wanted to hurry up and wait.

Sharon caught my eye and started to laugh with me, and soon, everyone was caught up in our second round of belly laughs. In the midst of our guffaws, LaKeemba nodded to Charlie, and he let memory go out into time.

The waiting had begun.

WE DIDN'T HAVE to wait long, though. In the time it took me to get to my feet and stretch, the wave of memory began to charge through the farm. First, we heard a wail, and I looked over to see Lizzie doubled-over with sobs. Alonso went to her at a run, and I followed as quickly as I could.

When I reached the young girl, she was phasing in and out of visibility, her memories causing her to lose control of her power. Alonso was holding on to her, and the longer he hugged her tight, the slower her invisibility phases became. Eventually, she sat down hard on the ground, and Alonso dropped with her. I leaned over, and that's when I heard her whisper, "Mama," over and over again.

But I didn't have time to figure out why the memory of her mother was so painful before chaos broke out around the farm and then beyond. Shouts bounced through the air, and down at the end of the farm lane, I thought I heard a car accident.

Mr. Wilson went running that way, and I headed toward the house to turn on the TV. A small part of me thought about turning on Netflix and bingeing *Longmire*, Mr. Wilson's favorite show, but I kept true to my purpose and turned on the news.

Chaos was breaking out everywhere. Car accidents, meals left to burn on stoves, even Three Mile Island, the nuclear power plant, went into emergency lockdown because the engineers were distracted from their work. In China, they had a pile-up of hundreds of bicycles when riders on the busy streets of Shanghai were distracted from their route. In Australia, a crew of opal miners was buried alive when they forgot to pay attention to the walls of the mine around them and hacked out an important support column. In Argentina, a massive commuter train ran off the tracks and into a small village on a mountainside because the engineer forgot to slow on the approach to a big curve.

As I watched, I felt the Wilsons and then LaKeemba, Sharon, and Alonso take seats beside me. Together, we saw horror after horror unfold on the screen, and when I tore my eyes away to look at my friends, I could see regret etched deep on all their faces as the blue-green of the TV screen flickered against their skin in the dark house.

What had we done?

JEDIDIAH

I'd had such a bad feeling about this—the kind of bad feeling that creeps up your neck and settles in the bottom of your ears. But I also knew, the way I sometimes just knew things, that we had to open that bottle. We had found it for a reason, and now, we had to figure out that reason.

The news stories were horrible to watch, but it was almost worse to see the reporters and anchors fight against their own memories to try and do their jobs. One reporter collapsed into a heap and rocked back and forth while holding her stomach and saying, "My baby, my baby," as actors from Broadway theaters streamed into the streets of New York in full costume because they were too overwhelmed to perform.

My own memories came slower now, Jennifer Cagle and the bruises on her arms, Sarah Beth healing up a gash I got from a barbed wire fence when I tried to rescue a puppy from a horse that was scared by the tiny, yipping creature, Mom singing to me in my crib. I was still seeing them, but they were less powerful and better, too, good memories for the most part.

I went to the kitchen and turned on the electric kettle so I could make everyone hot tea or cocoa. Normally, Mom would do this, but she didn't seem to be able to pull herself away from the television.

The water started to whistle, and as the sound filled my ears, I felt the memories recede a little, like the noise was taking up the space they'd held. I looked up at the clock and saw it had been over an hour since we—since I—opened the bottle, and a plan started to stretch itself in my mind.

I grabbed my sketchpad and sat down at the table after filling the kettle all the way to the top. I needed the water's squeal to keep going so I had enough bandwidth to draw this out.

First, I drew the kettle, then my parents and friends in the living room. Then, I drew the reporter on the sidewalk and the people in cat costumes behind her. I drew ships as they slammed into docks, and I drew abandoned ski lifts with people crying and stranded on the chairs.

I filled page after page of sketches. Sometime while I was drawing, Mavis came over. She looked at me, looked at the teakettle, and then filled it again. I gave her a quick thumbs up and went back to drawing.

Eventually, my sketches got lighter. Someone started the ski lift again, and ambulances arrived at accidents. It looked like people were waking up from a nightmare. Mavis watched over my shoulder, and when I started to draw smiling people, she put her hand on my shoulder and said, "I think that's something there, Jed."

I stared at my own pictures and nodded. "It's like the bad memories shoved their way out, but once they were gone, the good ones could get out, too."

Mavis sat down beside me. "Yeah, that's what it felt like to me. Like all the worst stuff was the strongest, so it pushed all the other memories to the back," she said.

I dropped my pen and stretched my fingers. "You think that means everything will be okay now?" I knew the answer already, but a tiny part of me hoped I was wrong.

"I wish," Mavis said with a sigh. "What's with the teapot?"

It was still wailing along behind us. "When the sound is going loud, I have more room in my head." I looked over at everyone by the TV. "They look better, even that far away." Mom and Dad were talking quietly on the couch, and Sharon and LaKeemba had stood up and stretched. Alonso was still watching the screen, but now, he didn't look like he might try to jump into it.

"Yeah, I think everybody's kind of coming back to themselves." She stood up and tugged on my elbow. "Let's go tell them what you figured out."

I stood to turn off the kettle when I heard my mom shout, "Look. Her."

When I spun toward the screen, I saw a little girl, a preschooler, standing on a busy street with people walking and bicycling around her. Her hands were out in front of her, her palms out as a huge delivery truck charged straight for her. The little girl's mother was behind her but facing the other direction, so she didn't see the danger.

But as we watched, the truck jerked to the right, like it had hit a slick force field, and the little girl dropped her hands.

"She has magic," Mavis whispered.

5

Mrs. Wilson sat for a long time as the camera followed the little girl and her mother. Eventually, a reporter interviewed the girl, and Alonso translated what she said. "I didn't do anything. The truck driver just turned the wheel."

Mrs. Wilson grabbed the remote and paused the DVR when the camera panned closer to the little girl's face. Mrs. Wilson sat, her eyes fixed on the little girl as if listening to more of what the child had to say.

I looked over at Jed, and he had the same sort of glazed look that his mom had. Mr. Wilson caught my eye and raised his eyebrows. I shrugged. I had no idea what was going on.

LaKeemba nodded toward the kitchen, and the rest of us headed toward the island, where Mr. Wilson got us some cheese and crackers and the glass bottles of soda the Wilsons kept for special occasions like birthdays. "We all need a little something extra tonight, I think," he said as he used the bottle opener to pop the lid on a cherry-flavored soda for Charlie.

Charlie looked pale and tired, but he smiled when Mr. Wilson handed him the bottle. "Thanks."

I looked back over at Jed and Mrs. Wilson. "What's with them?" I directed my question to LaKeemba, but I was just hoping anyone had an answer.

"They is seeing something," Sharon said. "The same something, I expect."

LaKeemba nodded. "I believe so. Magic usually travels in families, and I had long wondered when we would see Mrs. Wilson's gift come to the fore."

Mr. Wilson frowned. "What do you mean?" He looked back at his wife and son. "Are you saying that Jed got his gift from his mother?"

"I am, Leon." She put a hand on his arm.

His eyes turned back to the living room, and his head started to nod slowly. "This explains a lot."

"Like what?" I said a little too sharply and looked at Charlie. He shook his head. At least I wasn't the only one who didn't catch on.

"Well, like, Anna has always been able to say things other people were afraid to say, like the truth just comes out when she's around." He walked a few steps to the sink and stared out the window. "This one time, a man came by to look at some baby goats we had for sale. Anna didn't like the look of him, Jed neither, and he was just a few months old. He would not stop crying. Anna handed Jed to me and walked over to the man. 'You want all six of the kids we have?' she asked him. The man held up a stack of cash. 'Yes, ma'am. Take them off your hands this morning.'"

Mr. Wilson's face broke into a smile, and I could see the goats playing in the fields out the window. "She said, 'No, sir. We won't be selling to you today.' Then she turned and walked back to me. The man followed behind her, waving his money around. He was pointing at the soffits on the farmhouse that needed repairing and shouting about how we clearly needed the money. But Anna never looked back."

I felt a hand on my shoulder and turned to see Mrs. Wilson next to me. "I wasn't about to sell baby goats to a man who wanted to make a coat from their skin." She was grimacing. "Awful man."

"You just knew that's what he was going to do, Mom?" Jed asked.

"I guess I did. Knew it as soon as the man started talking, could hear it in his voice, maybe."

Quietly, LaKeemba said, "You see the secrets hidden behind words."

Mrs. Wilson looked over at LaKeemba. "Maybe. I just always thought that I had a good sense of people." Her eyes flitted back to the TV, where the little girl's face was still frozen. "But just now, I knew that little girl was lying, could just see the truth tucked between her words. She used magic, but she didn't want anyone to know."

All of us sat in silence, sipping our sodas for a bit. Another magic person. I liked that Mrs. Wilson was magic, but I also knew that usually powers only come this clear when they're needed. I didn't love that part.

Jed slapped the counter and tilted his head back, "Yahoo! Mama's magic, and we're going to India to get the girl from the TV."

I snapped my head to him. "We are?"

"Yes, Mavis. We are," LaKeemba said, and I stifled a groan.

For a long time, I had dreamed about traveling the world or even traveling off the farm. But I can honestly say that India had never been on my list of places to visit, as much as I loved the culture and, well, the food. I imagined the place to be dirty, over-populated, and chaotic. My attitude was terrible, but rather than just saying I didn't want to go, I tried to act all righteous. "I'll stay here and manage the farm, be sure things are in good shape and alert you all if something goes wrong."

Jed scowled. "You have to come," he said. "I need you to come."

Every eye in the room turned to me, and I wanted to shrug and say, "You'll be fine, Jed," but I had never been able to refuse that boy, not when he needed my presence. It was a core tenant of my existence in this world that I was Jed's companion, even though he was fifteen, even though I wasn't invisible to most of the world anymore. So I nodded.

A smile pulled at the corners of LaKeemba's mouth as she said, "We'll have folks here to keep an eye on things, Mavis. Don't worry."

I rolled my eyes. Sometimes I hated that I was such a terrible actor.

Our plans for travel were simple. We'd ride in the truck—Mr. and Mrs. Wilson, Jed, Charlie, LaKeemba, Sharon, Alonso, and I—a couple of towns over to an old oak tree that sat by the road where an abandoned farm once stood. It was one of the white oaks that had stood for hundreds of years. It was also our traveling ticket—the way we could move most easily through time and space. The magic people had scoped out the remaining trees in our area when they'd had to stop using their most precious one, which had been on the Wilsons' farm, because of a threat. These trees were the way that our friends travelled to help—and to escape. The fact that there was still one so close by was a gift, and the fact that it was on an abandoned piece of land but easily accessible, well, that seemed far more than coincidence.

I rode in the front of the pick-up beside Mrs. Wilson, who sat next to her husband as he drove us. Everyone else piled in the bed, and we hoped that they looked like a bunch of farmworkers on their way to a job so that the police would overlook how many laws we were violating.

As we pulled off the road and started up the trace of a lane to park the truck behind what was left of the farmhouse, I asked a question I hoped Mrs. Wilson would answer. "Why do we need to go?"

She stared out the windshield for a minute before looking at me. "She needs us. That's all I know."

I sighed. I guess I'd been hoping that the answer would be, "That little girl is the magical child who will save the world, and all we need to do is tell her that. Then, we can come home." But of course, it wasn't that simple, and when it wasn't that simple, I had learned, it was always not only more complicated but also more dangerous.

Alonso opened my door and held out a hand for me. I took it, and he squeezed my fingers. I smiled at him and decided I would enjoy this time with him, with all my friends, and think of it as an adventure. *It's an adventure. It's an adventure*, I chanted to myself, only half believing my own mantra.

We approached the tree and gathered in a circle. The key was that we all think of the same place so that we ended up there together. LaKeemba told us to think of the pinkish building behind the girl and to think of the girl just as she was in the news story. Those two images should fix us in time and space, but this part always made me so nervous.

With hands clasped, we walked one by one around the tree. Alonso went just before me, and I was last . . . which was why I was the only one to see the red-headed man as he ran toward the tree from the road. I screamed as I touched the tree and followed Alonso through space.

6

____

I was still screaming when I stepped out from behind the huge tree in what appeared to be a massive park. Alonso pulled me tight to his chest, both to comfort and to quiet me since people were beginning to stare.

"You okay?" he said into my hair.

I nodded, eager to tell someone about what I'd seen but even more eager to get away from the tree and away from Poke if he came around it. He wasn't supposed to be able to travel anymore, but I wasn't willing to take any chances.

I stepped away from Alonso and followed LaKeemba and Mrs. Wilson as they led us away.

We quickly moved out of the park and into the busy street nearby, trying to blend our white and black faces into the brown ones all around us. As we walked, people shifted to let us pass before closing the flow of people behind us again. We walked for several blocks, and I kept glancing behind me, watching. At least Poke's bright-red hair would stand out.

Ahead of us, I saw water, brown and huge, so much bigger than the James or Shenandoah, the rivers I knew from home. People were bathing in it and washing clothes in it, and while I could not imagine even wanting to put my toe in that water, I found myself enthralled by this place that felt, at least from first appearances, so different than home.

Mrs. Wilson and LaKeemba led us down a flight of stone steps to a stone walkway beside the river, and we slowed down. I huffed to a slower walk with gratitude and then sighed deeply when we stopped at a low wall to regroup. I clearly needed more aerobic exercise.

I tried to catch my breath to tell my friends who I'd seen back near the farm, but before I could speak, a man with a rich voice spoke from just above my shoulder. "This way, magic ones. Follow me."

I turned to look and saw an Indian man with a long white beard and coils of white fabric wrapped around his body standing above me. Well, at first I thought he was standing, but then I realized his feet weren't on the ground. He was levitating just enough that I could see the sky between his feet and the stone path on which he, um, didn't stand.

LaKeemba and Sharon exchanged a look, and Mrs. Wilson nodded. Without a word, we trailed down a long narrow alley behind the man, who was now walking. I'd have to remember that trick: if I needed to convince someone I was magic quickly, I could just do my disappearing thing. It's hard not to at least give someone the benefit of the doubt when they show you how much alike you are.

We wound back up to the main area of the city, but this time, we were staying off the larger streets. Our group of people twisted and turned through alleys so narrow we had to stay single-file. I tried to keep up with where we were going just in case . . . not all magic people were good, after all. But eventually, the series of rights and lefts confused me so badly that I had to take hope that we could get out if this were a trap.

Somehow, though, I didn't think so, and it wasn't just that LaKeemba typically had a really good sense of who we could trust or that Mrs. Wilson seemed to be able to tell when someone was lying. There was something about this man himself, something that reached me all the way back toward the end of our trail of people—only Alonso was behind me—that felt peaceful, hopeful.

Finally, the man led us through a stone arch and into the most amazing garden I had ever seen. We were surrounded by two- and three-story buildings made from the brown clay that most of the structures in this part of the city seemed to be made from, but every single wall was adorned with climbing flowers. The air smelled sweet, but not that too-sweet smell of the perfume some women wear, just a scent like peace and promise. Around us, there were beds full of shrubs and low mounds of flowers in purples and oranges, bright-yellows and reds. I felt like I'd walked into one of Mrs. Wilson's gardening magazines . . . with one exception. I could feel the magic in this place.

The air almost rippled with it. Every molecule of this space felt precious, charged like it could be called forth if we needed it, and as soon as we sat down on the circle of wooden benches in the center of the space, I felt like some weight I had been carrying for all my life slid down into the soil and fed the flowers around us. For a minute, I wondered if this was what the writer of Genesis had imagined when they'd written about the Garden of Eden.

We sat quietly for a moment, catching our breath, absorbing the beauty and the rest, but then I remembered Poke. My body started to tense again, but I couldn't speak yet. I turned to Alonso, and he smiled. "You saw something as we left?" he asked in the gentle voice he reserved for me.

I sighed and let the air of that place fill my lungs and circle my heart. "Poke. Poke was at the tree when we left." I turned to Charlie. "He's found us."

Charlie's face drained of blood, and despite the fact that he quickly sat on his hands, I saw that he was shaking. He only said one word, "How?"

It was the question I had been trying not to ask during our wanderings through the city. How could a man who could not travel in time make it from the nineteenth century to the twenty-first?

"I may have your answer, but first, let us know one another. We are safe here. No one but who we allow can enter. We have time." The man with the white beard's voice filled the space, and all my anxiety about Poke faded far back to the edge of my mind. "I am Davesh. My brothers and I keep this space as a refuge, a sanctuary for travelers. Be welcome here in our sanctuary and in Kolkata, our city."

I smiled at Davesh and realized that, despite the long beard, he was not as old as I had imagined. In fact, he looked quite young, hardly older than Charlie. He seemed kind but wise, and I wondered just how old he was. That magnificent beard didn't grow overnight, and I didn't know many eighteen-year-olds with white hair. Still, not much surprised me anymore.

Each of us shared our names with Davesh, and he greeted us each with a handshake that was somehow both firm and tender at the same time.

Then, he said, "Now, let us know more. Here is my trick." His eyes sparkled as he rose into the air and then dropped gently to the ground, like a dandelion seed carried by an air current. For a fleeting moment, I wondered if Santa used similar magic, but then, I remembered that Santa wasn't real.

We moved through our circle again, each of us giving a small display of what we could do. Sharon healed a small cut on Davesh's foot, and I flickered out of visibility and back in. Alonso placed his hand on Davesh's arm, and Davesh sighed as he said, "Ah, you are an enhancer."

Charlie paused time around a bright-orange flower that a bee was visiting, and we all leaned in to study the fuzzy back of the insect. Pollen dotted the creature, and I could have stared at it all day. It was so magical, just being itself.

Davesh then turned to Jed, and Jed let out a long stream of air through his lips before he spoke. He looked at LaKeemba, and she nodded.

"You have more power than you have shown us," Jed said.

Our host's eyebrows drew together, but he nodded as he said, "I do."

"My gift is to see secrets," Jed replied. "I just see them. I try not to judge them."

We had talked about that a lot—that having a gift that let you know things others didn't, didn't grant permission to try to change that person or even really do anything at all unless asked. It was a hard lesson to learn for someone like Jed, who just wanted to be helpful wherever he could.

Mrs. Wilson's voice was very, very quiet when she spoke, but I could hear her magic in it nonetheless. "I am a truth speaker." Her eyes darted to Sharon, who was smiling and nodding. Mrs. Wilson's ducked her head with embarrassment.

I couldn't help but to grin. She looked so happy.

Next, Mr. Wilson spoke. "I have no magic, but my power is to accompany those who do as help and comfort, and I would die for these people."

The strength in Mr. Wilson's voice brought tears to my eyes, and I wondered what it was like to be the sole person without magic in our merry band of travelers. I knew it would have bothered me something awful, but he looked peaceful, proud even.

Finally, only LaKeemba had not revealed her magic yet, and Davesh's face turned toward her as she spoke. "The way I serve is through the same power that protects this place. I cannot demonstrate my trick, as you call it, without disrupting your own."

A wide smile broke across Davesh's face. "You are our sister, then. You are all welcome as guests, but you, you are welcome to stay . . . if ever you should wish."

I watched LaKeemba's face, but as usual, I could read nothing on it. I couldn't imagine her leaving us, but then, I couldn't imagine most of the things that happened in the world now.

"Please, enjoy the garden. I will get us refreshment so we can be strong as we discuss what you have loosed on the world," Davesh said.

I gasped, but there wasn't any bitterness in the man's words or on his face. He was simply telling the truth, but I didn't like the sound of that. Not at all.

7

———

Jed looked at me and shrugged as he stood and walked off into the garden, his head bent to smell the flowers as he went. LaKeemba strolled off, too, and Sharon moved to a particularly colorful bed in one corner of the garden and began studying the petals there. Mr. and Mrs. Wilson were leaning against each other on a bench; their eyes closed as they rested together.

Alonso stood from his seat behind me and extended a hand. "Fancy a stroll?"

I felt color wash across my cheeks, but I didn't hesitate to take his hand, which he tucked into the bend of his elbow as we walked. He kept his fingers over mine, and I felt my blush deepen. I knew he and I would have a conversation about what was between us sometime, but now was not the time.

We walked a few more minutes. "What is this place?" I finally asked as we stopped by a bed of plants whose leaves were so glossy and deep green that they looked damp.

"The building is, I think, a monastery of sorts, and this garden, it's a medicinal garden, I believe." He scanned the plants around us.

"Ah, that's why Sharon is hoarding petals and leaves then." I nodded to the corner where she squatted with her small leather bag open.

Alonso chuckled. "I believe so. It is a good place; I'm sure of that. I can feel it. Can't you?"

I closed my eyes and let the air move around my face. "I can, I think. I don't feel nervous or scared here. I think that means it's a good place."

"I'm glad you feel safe and at peace here, Mavis. Very glad." He was looking intently at my face when I opened my eyes, and for one second, I thought he was going to kiss me. But then he turned toward an arched doorway just to our right as three men, including Davesh, brought out trays filled with the most amazing smelling food. It wasn't any Five Guys burgers—those things were *the best*, but the scents were incredible nonetheless.

Alonso and I made our way back to the center of the garden and saw that pillows had replaced the benches while we'd walked, but when I looked at the Wilsons, it appeared they hadn't changed position at all, like they'd been magically lowered to the pillows beneath them when their bench had been removed . . . and maybe they had.

The men set the trays of food in the middle of our circle, and I studied what was there as my mouth began to water. I saw samosas, fresh ones, not the frozen kind we sometimes ate at the Wilsons. Then, there were bowls of curry—yellow, red, and green. The paneer looked amazing, and the entire garden smelled rich with spice.

Davesh and the other two men sat down on cushions and then passed small plates to each of us before signaling us to help ourselves. I wanted to be the person who waited patiently while someone else went first, but I was so hungry. I leaned forward to put a spoonful of paneer and a samosa on my plate and bumped elbows with Alonso as he reached for the red curry. I laughed and then looked up and saw that all of us had reached for the food at the same time—no fake manners for us.

I settled back into my cushion and folded my legs under me, even though sitting on the ground was not my ideal for relaxation; my hips just hurt too much. But my discomfort disappeared as soon as I took a bite of that samosa. The warm potatoes, the crisp pastry, the spices made me sigh with delight. It was the best bite of food I'd ever tasted.

We ate in almost silence for a few minutes, the quiet of the garden interrupted only by our contented sounds. I think we could have stayed in that place eating that food for a very long time, but after a bit, Davesh called us back to ourselves with a single question. "May I see the bottle?"

He looked to Jed, knowing through that way most magic people have that Jed was its keeper, and Jed reached into his pocket, took it out, and handed it to our host. Davesh studied it for a moment and then slid the pad of his index finger over the etchings in the glass. "You read the warning but still opened it. Why?" His voice was kind but clear.

Jed looked first to his mother then to me. When we both nodded, he said, "Because we came to consensus," he smiled just a tiny bit when he used the new word for the first time, "that we had found it for a reason and needed to do something."

"And the only something you could think to do was open it?" The man to Davesh's right spoke for the first time, and I started. There was an edge to his voice, not of derision really but more of directness.

A look of shock passed through Jed's face, and I felt the same blast of worry fan through my chest, too. Maybe we had been too hasty. Was there something else we might have done?

"What else you think we could have done, sir? A sealed bottle. You either leave it be or open it up." Oh, I loved Sharon and her forthright speech.

The second man nodded. "Indeed. We are glad you came here now, even though we are not sure we would have done the same in your position." He bowed his head toward Sharon and then said, "I am Mohindor. I only ask my question to be sure you considered the choice carefully, not because I feel you made the wrong one." His eyes turned to LaKeemba.

"We made the best one we could with what we knew at the time," our leader's voice was low and steady as always. "All of us here know that time, sometimes, is a foe and sometimes a friend. We thought it wisest to act as if she was wending away from us and open the bottle soon. We hope we have done what was needed." She made eye contact with each of the three men seated across the circle from her, and they smiled.

"Well said, LaKeemba," the third man, to Davesh's left, said. "We never know what all our choices will bring, but we do what we can with what we do know. There will be—there have been —horrible consequences from this choice, but we must hope that the good will overcome that horror . . . and quickly."

"This is Aadrik. We are but three of the siblings who call this place home, but the others here have given us their consent to act as their voices. Too many people in a conversation like this can be overwhelming."

I nodded vigorously. I went to a county board of supervisors meeting a few weeks ago when there was a question about funding for the schools, and the room had been packed. Everyone wanted to say something and to be heard . . . but there was so much shouting and interrupting. I'd wanted to put my hands over my ears and lie down on the bench—too many people with too loud an agenda. I was glad that we were a small gathering this time.

"What about Poke?" I'd waited as long as I could with my question and my fear. I felt safe here, but our friends were back at the farm with that man so close by. I imagined Lizzie running into Poke and shuddered. "How is he in our time?"

"When you opened the bottle, you unleashed the bindings that held him to his place. The restrictions that had held him—and others like him—bound were loosed. He can now move freely." Davesh looked at me with concern in his eyes. "This Poke. I can see that he is someone you know, someone you fear."

Alonso spoke, "He has harmed us before, so yes, we fear him. More, we fear what he might do now, though, to us but to others as well. This is one of those unintended consequences, I suppose."

Mohindor nodded. "Yes, but we do not yet know whether it will be for good or for ill. That, we must determine." He stood. "But first, I believe you came to meet someone in particular." He turned his eyes toward Mrs. Wilson, and she rose to stand in front of him. "Let me take you to Lili."

"Prepare yourselves," Davesh said. "The first porting can be a bit disorienting."

I only had time to look at Jed and then feel Alonso's hand grab mine before Mohindor raised his arm to the sky and everything went swirly.

JEDIDIAH

I'm not quite sure what I expected for my first time teleporting, but whatever I'd thought was going to happen didn't, because we just went from one place to another without much of nothing. For a second, everything around me looked like that stuff in the old lava lamp Dad kept out in his office in the barn, but then, we were just standing somewhere else in Kolkata. I felt like maybe TV shows made too much of that whole process what with the tunnels of laser beam thingys and stuff.

I did think it would be cool to do it, though. I could teleport to get a coke or to get to school, and if I were like Mohindor, I could take Charlie with me, and we could get to the bike trails up in the park without having to wait for Mom or Dad to drive us. Teleporting had its privileges, I thought to myself with a giggle.

I stopped laughing right quick, though, when Mom caught my eye. She had the stare Charlie and I called "the death look." She didn't give it to me often, but when she did, I knew I better straighten out, or I'd be in for a very, very long lecture when we got home. Nothing was worse than one of Mom's lectures about being a good person. They could go on for hours and meant I had to listen to all her stories again.

The smile dropped from my face, and I turned to see how Mavis had fared from the trip. She was a bit green, and she had her arm across her mouth like she might throw up. But Sharon was giving her a little vial of something that I expected would make her feel right better. Plus, Alonso had his arm around her like he did a lot now, and she was leaning into him. She'd be fine in a minute.

When Dad had first asked me how I felt about Mavis dating Alonso, I'd said, "What are you talking about?" Mavis almost never left the farm, even though she could now, and I knew she and Alonso hadn't ever been on a date. But then I thought about how they were always taking walks and sitting together when all of us ate, and I realized what Dad meant. I hadn't really answered Dad's question then because, at first, the idea of Mavis with Alonso had made my belly burn a little. I guess I was jealous, maybe, or something. But after thinking about it a couple of weeks, I realized I didn't need Mavis the way I used to when I was a kid, and maybe she did need Alonso, someone to be hers in a way. So I tried to just be happy for her, even though I missed her sometimes.

Now, though, I was glad she had other people to take care of her. She gave me a little wink when she caught me staring at her, and I knew she'd be okay. Good thing, too, because just then, that little girl came out of a house beside us, and everything went a little wild.

8

Thank goodness for Sharon's elixir because I was really going to make quite a messy scene there on that street without it. Teleporting was not, I knew, ever going to be my favorite means of transport. Time traveling was disorienting enough, but then, I moved myself. To be whisked through the air like a frisbee . . . well, I didn't even have much time to think about it because when the girl from TV came out on the street, the air shifted as if a giant machine had stepped in front of us. I had to brace myself against Alonso's shoulder to keep from taking a step back.

Somehow, I knew it was important not to step back, and all the rest of my friends must have known the same because we were all braced with our legs wide and our hands beside us. The force of her was amazing, especially because she was so tiny. Her head was barely as high as my waist, and she could clearly have used some of the cooking from Davesh's sanctuary. But from her pounded this energy, this something—I didn't know what words to use to describe it—that felt like ocean waves mingled with jet engines.

"Lili," Davesh said. "These people are friends. We are here

to help." He knelt down in front of the girl and stretched out a hand to her.

Her deep-brown eyes met his, and I lurched forward, the weight of her power suddenly gone.

"Friends?" she whispered. "Not scary people." She gave her head a vigorous shake.

"Not scary people," Davesh whispered as Lili stepped forward and climbed onto his knee. "We are here to help."

Mrs. Wilson walked slowly forward and sat down beside Davesh. "I'm Anna," she said, and I thanked whatever magic made it always possible for us to understand people in places where we didn't know the language. "I saw you from far away, and I knew we needed to come to you. Can you tell me what is happening?"

Lili's eyes grew wide, and she started to shake. But Davesh pulled her tighter to himself. "Bad people took my mama. They took her far away." Tears pooled in her eyes, but I could tell she was trying to keep from crying. "Can you help me?" She stood up and climbed over into Mrs. Wilson's lap.

And that did it. I couldn't keep from crying myself then.

"Oh, yes, we will try to help. What's wrong, Lili?" Mrs. Wilson's voice had taken on the soft, lilting tones of every woman caring for a person in need. But behind her words, there was more, more than just the natural instinct to comfort. In her speech was magic, and the instant it came forth, Lili's face softened.

"I'm tired," the little girl said, and her eyes started to stay closed longer with each blink. "I can't hold them back much longer." Her voice was slow now, and in a moment, she was asleep.

"Prepare, my new friends. They are coming." Mohindor said crisply.

As usual, I wanted far more information about what was happening. How did I prepare? What was I preparing for?

Shouldn't we just run? But all I had time to do was brace myself and take Alonso's and Jed's hands in mine as we formed a circle around Lili and Mrs. Wilson.

Then, they arrived. Invisible or maybe bodiless screams that charged through the air like a horse whipped to a frenzy. The sound made me feel like I wanted to let my mind slip away deep in itself to a place where no one could ever reach me again. If my friends hadn't been there, hadn't been using their magic to protect us, I might have done just that.

Instead, though, I felt the wave of magical power ripple through us, and the voices backed away as if we were a dam set against a rushing river. We couldn't hold them forever, but we had them now.

"Tell me where we are going. Give me one image, something specific," Mohindor shouted above the roar of the screams.

Somewhere behind me, Mr. Wilson said, "A 1987 Bronco, blue and white, license plate RSC-8895." It was a brilliant choice to describe his car, and in a swirl of gut-wrenching movement, we were there, back at the farm, just as it had been when we'd left it. Awkwardly, however, Alonso and I had ended up on the top of the Bronco, holding hands. Alone.

Out of instinct, I tried to pull away, but Alonso clenched his fingers tighter around mine. "Let them look, Mavis. It's fine," he whispered.

Lizzie came running when she saw us by the barn where Mr. Wilson always parked, and I saw a grin flash across her face as she got closer and saw our hands twined together. But that smile quickly passed when she saw our faces. "I'll gather everyone."

Alonso helped me climb down, and then, we stood, all eleven us who had just returned, staring at one another until Davesh asked the oddest question possible, "Have you read *Harry Potter*?"

Some small part of wanted to be a smart aleck and say,

"Who hasn't?" And another part of me wanted to scoff at him for asking such an absurd question, but fortunately, the larger part of me was still too nauseous from our quick trip to actually form words.

"I have. Why?" Charlie's voice was skeptical.

"You know the dementors then," Davesh answered.

Many heads nodded. Jed's copies of the books had made their way around the yurts shortly after Charlie had finished each. They were instant favorites because of the magic, because of the friendship, because they felt like—in some real way—that they told our story. We'd even had informal book clubs to talk about each title. We knew these books well.

"Of course," Jed said, and I could hear both the wariness and the interest in his voice. "Why?"

"What you just heard," Davesh continued, "were the voices of those who died in horrible ways, ways people don't want to remember. Like the dementors, they have been twisted by their greatest desire—to have their stories told and remembered."

Again, I was writhing under the weight of my eleventy million questions, but I waited.

"In India, those voices belong to people who died of hunger or disease or disability because they were too poor to be cared for." Mohindor's eyes fixed on the tree line at the back of the farm. "They are the people our system of castes forgot on purpose."

"Like the people who Mother Theresa helped," Mrs. Wilson said from the hood of the Bronco, where she and Lili sat, still entwined.

"Yes, and the people who lived for centuries before." Mohindor climbed up onto the hood. "When memory was unleashed, they came into power. Now, their voices can be heard, and they are demanding their due."

Lili let out a shuddering sigh, and I noticed she was still asleep. She hadn't even woken up, it seemed, on the trip.

"Lili had been holding them at bay for the city, knowing they were too many for people to handle. Too much rage behind all that wanting," Davesh said with a long sigh. "She protected us from ourselves." He ran a light finger over the little girl's hair as he leaned against the Bronco's side.

I couldn't wait any longer. The question burning in my throat needed to be spoken, but I took a breath and formed my thoughts with care, not just my own need. "I understand what you're saying, and I'm so sorry those people suffered. So sorry that their suffering is haunting your city. Still, there has been great suffering everywhere, why aren't we hearing from those unremembered here?"

"The Unremembered. That is a wonderful phrasing, Mavis," Mohindor said. "They are here, too, I'm sure. As you said, the crushing pain of history's trauma lives everywhere. I can only guess that because of this open space, they have not rushed here because they want more people to hear their cries." He turned his gaze across the farm. "They will come, though."

The rest of the people from the yurts were walking toward us now, Lizzie leading the way, and LaKeemba said, "We must gather. We have two great needs, and we must marshal all our forces."

And like a blow to my gut, I remembered Poke and turned to see Charlie's face blanch with fear for the second time.

9

———

When we had all gathered on the sloping pasture near the barn, LaKeemba climbed up on the tractor so that she could see us all, meet our eyes. There must have been about thirty-five of us then. We'd had some of our friends move on from the farm over the last couple of years, ready to live in the regular American society, but we'd also had a few people join us because they'd needed respite, recovery, or just the quiet, a space to just be their magic selves. Everyone on the farm gathered, and I had the impression that even the goats and chickens were listening.

"There is an expression that rises up from the throats of people who mean well but still value their way, their perspective, their place more highly than that of others. They say they are being a 'voice for the voiceless.' Their intentions are good—justice, compassion, teaching—but their basic premise is flawed. No one is voiceless. Even those who can't speak have ways of making themselves heard."

I took a deep breath and thought about the times I had imagined myself a champion, a hero for people who were helpless. That feeling had made me feel good, righteous. I had felt like my work was what was saving those people. Now, I just felt embarrassed.

"People are never voiceless, but they are often silenced. Silenced by other people. Silenced by systems and practices that mute their voices, take away their power, rob them of choice." LaKeemba's voice was strong and clear, and I could see many of my friends nodding. They had been silenced. They knew what she was talking about. "Our job is not, then, to speak for people but to remove the things that silence them. Our job is to listen, to listen and then to amplify, too."

Behind me, Davesh and Mohindor were smiling. I imagined that back in Kolkata, they were the ones giving this kind of speech.

"Among us now are the Unremembered. We aren't hearing them yet, but we have been told they will come. We must be ready. Ready to listen and then ready to make their voices heard further."

For a minute, I had this vision of all of us becoming a huge speaker that we could turn in a full circle, the memories of those forgotten blasting through us. I wasn't sure I liked that image, but I was sure that my preferences didn't matter much here.

LaKeemba's voice grew softer now. "We must show these Unremembered people that we hear them, and we must help other people hear, too." She turned to face Charlie. "But we must also show those who wish to forget, those who have actively fought to silence people that we will not tolerate their actions any longer."

Charlie held LaKeemba's gaze, and then he gave one, crisp nod. I felt tears gather in my throat. That boy, that young man was so strong.

"But how?" Lizzie's voice echoed off the barn walls, and I nodded. She was asking my question, too.

LaKeemba smiled. "Ah, that is both the simplest and

hardest part of all. We do this work in our own ways with our own gifts. We will each have our way and our part, and it will require who we are and what we have. But nothing more."

Nothing more? I thought. What more is there besides who I am?

"Now, though, we rest. We gather our strength together. We ready ourselves." A smile cracked across her face. "We are ready, friends. We are made for this. Take heart. We are ready."

I wanted to believe her. In some deep part of myself, near the center of my chest, I could hear the truth of what she said. I was ready. But the rest of me, my hips and hands and especially my head, the rest of me had its doubts. Still, I knew nothing else to do but believe LaKeemba and try to trust myself and my friends.

I WALKED BACK to my yurt. I was looking forward to my bed and rereading a little *Harry Potter* as a distraction. But I had only just gotten under the covers when I heard a sound, a rustling from the drawer in my nightstand. I groaned.

I really wanted to ignore the noise and leave that drawer closed. But LaKeemba's words echoed inside my brain—I had to do what I was made to do, and that sound was a reminder about part of what I was made for. Inside the drawer was a folded piece of paper, a map that let me see things other people couldn't see, a map that let me travel through time and space without the need of old trees.

I closed my eyes and opened the drawer, reaching my hand in with my eyes still shut. I picked up the heavy paper and unfolded it on my lap without opening my eyes. Then, I took a deep breath and looked down.

There, at the center of the page, was the farm. I could see the golden glow that always showed me home. Now, the glow was bright, almost like a light in the page itself, and I realized that the light was always brighter when more of the people who made my home were gathered. More of us were gathering here, the map revealed. More were returning. I smiled and stood up just as Shelby knocked on my door.

Shelby had been gone a few months, off to find her own way. "I just need a break, Mavis. A little space to figure out who I am on my own. You all are so shiny that sometimes I just can't quite see myself, you know?" That's what she'd told me the day she had left, and I didn't get it. For so long, I had wanted to be seen, to be known, that I didn't understand leaving the people who knew you. But I loved Shelby, and if she needed that, then I wanted her to have it.

To see her back now, though, just her face made me smile, and I felt that tiny spot of confidence in my chest grow a little bigger.

"Miss me?" she said, and I leapt to hug her.

"You're back!" I said into her shoulder as she held me tight.

"For a visit. But yes, I'm back." Shelby's face was joyful when I stepped away to look at her.

"I'll take it."

Shelby had left a couple of months ago, but it felt like she'd been gone for years.

I had been so sad when she'd left, but I had really hoped she'd find what she needed. I also had secretly hoped she'd find it here, after she explored a little. "How was your trip?"

She plopped down on my bed and drew her knees up to her chest. "Amazing, Mavis. I saw so many places, met so many people." Then, she held my gaze. "I found a place, Mavis. A place where I can just let myself be."

I smiled, even though I felt a little heartbroken, too. She wasn't coming home, but she had found her home. That was not something small. I knew that myself. "Where is that?"

"Oh, you'll have to come visit so I can show you. I think

you'll like it there, too." Her smile was soft, and I realized that for the first time since I'd known her, Shelby looked peaceful.

I smiled back and started to sit down next to her just as she jumped back to her feet. "But right now, we have something we need to take care of. You saw him, right?"

My stomach zoomed back up to my mouth as I thought about Poke. I nodded. "Up at the white oak by the abandoned Ferguson place." I told her what Davesh had said about how opening the bottle had freed him to travel again. Then I looked deep into her eyes and said, "I think he's here for Charlie."

"I think so, too, but ahead of us, he doesn't have him. It doesn't feel good up there, though." Her gaze had softened like it always did when she was looking into the future. "I see nothing specific yet, which means it's not settled, but there's a darkness. A shadow."

As her eyes came back into focus, she said, "It's back, Mavis."

10

———

As Shelby and I left my yurt to see Jed in the farmhouse, we were mostly silent. I couldn't get any words to come to my mouth as I thought about The Shadow that had almost consumed us and an entire town last summer. The thing fed on hopelessness, fear, and secrets.

We'd defeated it once, but it had taken more magic than we even knew we had. And even then, we had only been able to force it to retreat, not destroy it altogether. Now, not only had we made it possible for Poke and all of his human evilness to come to us, but The Shadow was also lurking. I kind of wanted to give up now, maybe go back to being imaginary. I just didn't see how we could win.

"The question is, what does Poke want Charlie for?" Shelby said quietly as we reached the farmhouse porch. She turned to me. "Or I guess really the question is, why does he want Charlie to stop time?"

My heart lurched. She was right. Charlie had some of the most powerful magic among us, and it seemed most likely that Poke had a reason for coming for Charlie—if that's why he was here; we were still guessing. That reason wasn't love; we knew that. That man had never shown that boy an ounce of love.

Shelby and I looked at each other for a minute, and I took the map out of my pocket. "She's moving around again," I said as I felt the paper rustle in my fingers.

"Oh," Shelby said as she looked down at my map. "Just the map, though?"

I thought of the powerful goddess who had once embodied the map and then me when the map first came to my hands. She had left, but the map still carried magic. I nodded. "Just the map, but she's stronger, I think." Then I shook my head. "I don't know what I'm saying. Maybe I'm just holding onto anything that can help."

"Sounds like that's the best thing in the world, Mavis," Mrs. Wilson said as she came around the corner of the house, a watering can in her hand. "We need all the help we can get." She swung open the farm door. "Shelby, I'm so glad to see you. Let's get some tea."

At the thought of Mrs. Wilson's sweet sun tea, I felt a little more hope bloom in my chest. Sharon was always saying that food healed, and I was a firm believer in that, especially when it came to iced tea and maybe hush puppies, too. I loved a warm hush puppy fried just right with that crispy outside and that warm cornbread middle. When this was all over, I was going to perfect my hushpuppy skills, I decided.

Mrs. Wilson poured three glasses of tea and added ice to each glass before sitting down. "Shelby, I'm glad to see you for many reasons, but today, I need your help especially. I think I just had a vision."

Shelby smiled but didn't look surprised. Very little surprised Shelby. "Alright, then. Tell me about this vision."

Mrs. Wilson took a long swig of her tea and then said, "We are all together, all of us from this place plus more folks, folks with magic, and we're holding hands. Some of us are telling stories, and some of us are listening. Some of us are singing, some dancing, some praying. Mavis, you're there in the middle, and you have the map. Jed is there, too, and he's drawing in the air, big, wild visions that look like both the future and the past. Charlie is beside the two of you, but he's the only one not doing anything." She took another sip of her tea. "But he looks so happy, so peaceful."

The kitchen around us grew heavy with quiet, and we sat still, letting that vision fill the room. Somehow, just the idea of us together made me braver, and I knew in the way I just know true things sometimes that the idea of us being together was crucial, central to what's coming. I also knew there was more.

Finally, Shelby drew a long, slow breath and then drummed her fingers on the table one time. "Well, that is definitely a vision. I can tell you a bit about how mine work, but I think this one is pretty clear, right?"

I looked at Mrs. Wilson, expecting her to nod because it seemed really clear to me, too, but Mrs. Wilson was shaking her head. "No, it's not clear at all. I don't know where we are. I don't know how we get there. I don't know what I'm supposed to do with what I've seen."

Shelby put a hand on Mrs. Wilson's arm. "Ah, but that's not your part. Your part is the telling. You leave the doing to the people who do that part."

Mrs. Wilson's brow furrowed, and she looked from me to Shelby.

"Would it help you if I told you what your vision tells me?" I ask.

"Yes, it would, please." Mrs. Wilson's voice was almost pleading.

"I see us all together. I see each of us doing what we do. I see us protecting Charlie." I smiled. "And I see Charlie happy. That might be the most important part." I looked at this woman I'd known for years, this woman who had always seemed to have it all together, and she looked scared. So I took her other hand in mind. "This helps, Mrs. Wilson. This helps me just now. Knowing we will do this together, that I don't have to do it alone, that I don't have to figure it all out. That helps so much. I feel braver just knowing that you will all be there, wherever and whenever *there* is."

Mrs. Wilson smiled at me then, and I saw a little of her fear drop away. The map was sitting beside me on the table, and I heard her rustle. All three of us turned to look at the paper, and as we did, she started to unfold herself. I moved the tea glasses out of the way and tugged her over between us on the table.

There, not far from where we were sitting, was a blue glow, the glow that told me this was where we needed to go. Charlottesville, a city just over the mountains. "See, there's your *where*, Mrs. Wilson. That's where we need to gather."

Shelby stood up and reached down to help first me and then Mrs. Wilson to our feet. "Then, let's go tell everyone."

We headed out the door to find LaKeemba.

JEDIDIAH

I wasn't quite sure what to think when Mom said she'd had a vision. She looked happy and a little scared, and I was excited for her—kind of. But also, I mostly just wanted her to be my mom, to do things to help me. I know that's selfish, but it's the truth. I tried to be support- ive, though, because I knew that was better, even if it was harder.

Mavis's map was glowing again, and she was smiling. In fact, everyone was smiling after Mom described what she saw, even me. I had only drawn in the air that one time, and it had worked to push back The Shadow. I was excited to do it again. I was nervous, too, though, because I didn't know what I needed to draw. Sharon reminded me that the "what" would become clear in the moment. "Always does," she whispered.

We were around the firepit again, this time with marshmallows. Apparently, Davesh and Mohindor had never seen a marshmallow, let alone enjoyed the delicacy of one slightly torched by a campfire. They quickly understood how amazing they were, and I think Davesh ate like ten. I tried to warn him, but he would not be stopped.

LaKeemba had listened to what Mom and Mavis knew, and then Shelby had added that she thought we needed to move quickly, that her sense was that tomorrow was the day. It was good to see Shelby again, but man, I wished we could just relax when we were all together for once.

Since things were moving fast, LaKeemba asked Davesh and Mohindor if they could please return to their home and bring back anyone who might help. Lili was going to stay with us, but Mohindor would bring her mom back tonight—if he could free her—so that Lili knew she was safe. We'd waited until now just in case it didn't go well. We didn't want to tip our hand. "You'll be glad she's here," he'd said mysteriously just before he disappeared.

Next, Lizzie and Alonso were sent out to call or text everyone we knew and ask them to meet us in Charlottesville the next morning. "Nine a.m., right, Shelby?" LaKeemba asked.

"That's the time I see," Shelby said, and Alonso and Lizzie stepped away with their phones in hand.

It was only then that I realized Charlie wasn't there by the fire, and for a minute, my heart jumped into my throat. Then, I saw him, over by the barn with one of the cats twirling around his legs. I pointed him out to Dad, and Dad said, "Go. I'll take notes for you."

I waved as I walked over to Charlie. He was leaning against the barn wall, so I joined him and then let myself slide down until I was crouched between the ground and the building. Charlie picked up the cat, Tinkerbell, and slid down next to me.

"You okay?" I asked.

Charlie shrugged. "I am alive and healthy."

I looked at him sideways. "You know that's not what I meant."

"I know." He petted Tinkerbell a few times. "I may need you to convince me not to do something."

"What do you need me to convince you not to do?" I wanted to jump up and go ask my dad for help because this felt big, too big for me. Too big for Charlie. But then I looked at us, both of us tall, thin, and I remembered how my mom had studied us last week when we were helping her plant herbs for her garden. She'd said, "My two young men." I took a deep breath.

"I just want to stop time around us and keep us here, prevent anything else from happening. I don't want anything to change further." Charlie pulled the cat tight to his chin and buried his face in her fur.

I understood what he meant. I wished things weren't changing too, for lots of reasons. Mostly I was tired of people leaving. I mean, I was glad Shelby was back, but I almost wish she'd stayed away so I didn't have to say goodbye to her again. "I get it." I looked over at Charlie. "But you know you can't do that, right? All those other people, we have to help them."

"Why?" Charlie stood up, and Tinkerbell leapt away. "Why is it my responsibility to take care of everyone else? Why can I not just take care of the people I love?" His voice got quiet then. "Of the people who love me?"

I sighed. I didn't have a good answer. Mom and Dad had taught me to care about everyone, and I tried. But sometimes it was exhausting. Sometimes it felt like I was last on the list. Sometimes I just didn't have it in me to help everybody.

Charlie ran his fingers through his red hair and groaned. "But we made this mess, did we not? We opened the bottle."

"Technically, I opened the bottle."

He rolled his eyes. "We opened the bottle. We have to deal with the consequences." He looked over at our friends up the hill. "I will not be like my father. I will not pretend that things must be this way and that I had nothing to do with how they got here. I will not."

Evening was starting to settle in around us, and the sky had turned a light purple. I smiled. "I think you pretty much convinced yourself, huh?"

Charlie huffed. "I suppose."

"Yeah, you did because I didn't even have to tell you about Mom's vision to convince you."

"Your mom had a vision?" he said as he pushed off the barn wall toward the gathering.

"She did. We were all together, working, except you. You were in *the middle of us all, watching and smiling." I patted him on the shoulder as we began to walk up the slope. "You were happy."*

A slight smile flashed across his lips as we walked toward the fire.

11

For the first time in one of our undertakings, there wasn't a lot of planning to do. We didn't need assignments or travel plans. There were no costumes or elaborate ruses to disguise our actions. Nope, this time we were going in together with just our magic, and I was comforted . . . also terrified. But when wasn't I terrified?

The night was nice, though, one of those cool evenings of spring when a fire is the perfect thing to keep off the dew.

Sharon was singing, her head thrown back. "God's gonna trouble the water."

I hummed along quietly as I watched the fire.

Charlie and Jed were laughing and threatening each other with burning sticks. Lizzie was dancing in the firelight, and the rest of us just listened and watch. It was a peaceful moment, so peaceful I could almost forget we were going to battle in the morning.

Alonso sat down next to me and put his arms around my shoulder, pulling me close. I shut my eyes and leaned into him.

"You okay?" he asked.

I took a deep breath and thought about my answer a second. "I am. Scared. But alright."

He kissed the top of my head. "I'd probably be worried if you weren't frightened. I'm glad you're alright, though." He paused and squeezed me a bit tighter. "I have a good feeling about tomorrow."

I pulled back and looked up into his face. "You do? You a prophet now? Because we already have two of those. I think we're set." I grinned, and he rolled his eyes.

"Nope, no prophecies here. Just confidence in us. In what we can do."

I looked around the circle and felt the same thing. We weren't perfect. We weren't the Avengers with our honed skills and slick costumes. But we were strong, especially together. I could feel that in the air around us.

I rested my head back on Alonso's shoulder and watched the fire.

A BIT LATER, Mohindor appeared behind LaKeemba. A young Indian woman was beside him.

"Lili's mom?" I whispered to Alonso.

"Yes, and Mohindor was right. We will be glad she is here."

I sat up. "Oh, why is that?"

"I'm not sure yet, but she has some of the strongest magic I've ever felt. If you try, I bet you can feel it, too."

I closed my eyes and lifted my chin. At first, I didn't feel anything except the gentle pulse I felt whenever magic people were together, but then, just at the edge of my perception, I noticed it, a richer thrum. It reminded me of those monks who sing in that deep voice that sounds almost like a moan. The feeling vibrated against my ribs, and it felt amazing.

The small woman stood very still and watched all of us. Then a bright smile broke across her face as Lili ran toward her.

The two of them hugged and whispered for a while before Lili turned to us and spoke, "This is my mama."

Lili's mother faced all of us, her eyes moving slowly over every face, and she said, "I'm Mayuri. Thank you for taking care of Lili." Then, she collapsed.

WITHIN A FEW MINUTES, Sharon and Alonso had carried Mayuri to Sharon's yurt with Davesh, Lili, and me trailing behind. I didn't know if I could help, but I thought maybe Lili might need to be distracted. I picked up small twigs as I walked across the field. Jed and I had made many a long summer afternoon shorter by playing impromptu games of pick-up sticks. I didn't have much else to offer, but I could give a child the pleasure of winning something fair and square. I was so bad at pick-up sticks that Lili was sure to win.

Mayuri was resting on Sharon's bed by the time I reached the yurt, and Lili was sitting on Davesh's lap at Sharon's small dining table. I sat across from them and watched Sharon work for a few minutes. Lili's eyes were wide with fright, but after she'd had enough time to see that Sharon, who was singing and resting her hands on Mayuri's belly, and Alonso, who was giving Sharon some extra strength, weren't going to hurt her mom, I said, "One time, Sharon healed Jed's broken arms just by singing over them. She'll help your mom."

Lili glanced at me and then back over at Sharon again. "I know. Her magic is tingly, and tingly is good."

"You can feel magic?" I said.

"You can't?" Lili turned to me and spoke with just the slightest bit of disbelief mixed with sass. I took that as a good sign.

I looked down at the pile of sticks by my fingers. "Well, I can sort of. I could feel when your mom came, and I can feel it sort of like it's a breeze. But not really much else." I looked up at her. "How does it feel to you?"

Lili was watching me now, and I pushed the pile of sticks into the center of the table. "Want to play?"

When she nodded, I explained how we had to pull one stick out without moving any of the others. She went first and took a tiny twig out of the middle of the pile without moving any of the others. She was definitely going to win.

"Does everybody's magic feel different to you?" I asked as I took my turn and miraculously managed to remove a stick.

She slid a twig out of the pile with ease and said, "Yeah. Like yours is all swimmy, like sunshine on water."

My eyes flicked up to hers. "You can feel that I have magic?"

"Oh yes," she said as she tilted her head. "It's pretty."

I smiled then. "Thank you."

Davesh looked at me and nodded as he shifted Lili to the chair and leaned down to say, "I'm going to go help the others. Mavis will stay with you, and I'll just be by the fire if you need me."

Lili didn't take her eyes off the pile of sticks as I took the easy way out and picked up one of the ones on top. "What does Alonso's magic feel like?" I tipped my head toward him by the bed.

"Like mine," she said quietly. "Like a magnet."

I thought about that description a moment as I watched Lili navigate a thick stick from under two others. Lili's power was to hold things back, and Alonso's was to amplify power . . . maybe they sort of worked in the same way. I made a mental note to ask Alonso about that sometime.

We continued to play for a while until, as I expected, I moved the pile and lost. Lili looked up at me and smiled, "Good game," she said.

"Why, thank you, Lili." We both looked over at the bed,

where Sharon was singing softly with her hands on Mayuri's belly. "What does your mother's power feel like, Lili?"

"Like the ocean." Her words came fast and clear. She knew, and that description seemed perfect to me. Mayuri's magic was vast and deep; even I could feel that.

Lili and I played a couple more games of pick-up sticks, and she won every time. Eventually, though, we just sat in silence and watched Sharon and Alonso work. There was a quiet rhythm about Sharon when she healed, a gentleness that most people didn't notice in her normally. It was a beautiful thing, and it made me love my friend more.

Alonso's gift was more subtle—like he was, I guess—but no less powerful. He moved with Sharon easily, keeping a hand between her shoulder blades so that her healing magic was stronger than it would have been on her own. Every once in a while, he looked over at me and smiled, but mostly, he concentrated on passing strength to Sharon while she healed Mayuri.

After a bit, I saw Mayuri stir, and Lili jumped up and ran to hold her mother's hand. Mayuri's eyes fluttered open, and she smiled at her daughter. "I am okay," she said.

I felt tears on my cheeks. I was relieved that Mayuri was improving, but I also loved that the first thing she said comforted her little girl.

Sharon helped Mayuri sit up, and I rushed to get all three of them cups of strong tea that I had brewed while they worked. I'd seen Sharon do enough healing to know that she needed sustenance immediately to replenish, and this tea—a blend Shelby made—was her go-to drink after a healing session.

I slipped a pillow behind Mayuri's back and then handed her the tea. Lili climbed up into the bed beside her.

"Can you tell us what happened?" I asked Mayuri gently, not wanting to push but sensing that we needed to know.

I saw a shadow cross the threshold of the door and glanced over. Charlie and Jed had come in with LaKeemba. They all stood quietly at the foot of Sharon's bed while Mayuri sipped from her mug. The color was coming back under her skin, and she was breathing more softly.

After a few minutes, she sat up a little straighter and then looked at Charlie. "He must be your father," she said.

I whipped my head from her to Charlie, expecting to see surprise on his face, but he didn't look anything but sad. "He is," he said. "He hurt you?"

The expression on Mayuri's face hardened just slightly, but her eyes stayed soft as she spoke again. "He did, but what he does is not yours to bear. I do not hold you responsible. You are your own man."

I tried not to make any noise as I choked back a sob. I knew Charlie needed to hear what she said, and when I looked at him, it seemed like maybe he had heard that truth for the first time. Sharon and LaKeemba had told him the same on several occasions—that he did not carry the guilt of his father's awfulness, just the responsibility that all of us shared to make things right. But the weight of Poke's legacy had been a yoke around Charlie's neck for a long time.

Now, though, I saw something in his jaw go soft ever so slightly, and I thought about how much the kindness of strangers can change us. The ugliness of them, too.

"They kept me in a room full of papers, here in America, I think. I could hear people speaking English like you do." She turned her gaze to me. "Where all the vowels are long and some of the final consonants missing."

I grinned. "They had southern accents?"

She nodded. "I believe so. They wanted me to use my power, but I refused."

Lili slid even closer to her mother as if she knew what was coming next required comfort for both of them.

"They showed me horrible things," Mayuri's eyes darted down to her daughter and then back up to Sharon, "terrible things from history. I don't even want to describe them, but I have seen them before in books and films. The camps in Germany. The plantations here. Coups in Haiti and Argentina. The gulags of Russia. The broken treaties of the American West."

I knew of all these things myself from books. These were some of the places of harshest violence in the world's history, moments when humans had done horrible things to one another, murdered one another by the thousands, sometimes by the millions. I could understand why she wouldn't want to tell the details of what she saw, not with Lili there.

LaKeemba spoke. "They wanted you to take us back there?"

Mayuri nodded. "My magic is the ability to shift time, to move people through it."

Charlie gasped. "Another time worker?" His eyes were wide, and I couldn't tell if I saw hope or fear in his eyes. "Like me."

Jed put his arms around Charlie's shoulders. "You refused to do what your dad wanted. You're like her that way, too."

"Why? Why did he want you to take us back?" Charlie sat down on the bed and pulled at the tufts on the handmade quilt.

"He said he wanted to make things right, to stop those terrible things from happening," Mayuri said.

I turned to meet Alonso's gaze because I couldn't imagine Poke wanting to do anything that served anyone besides himself. He was a selfish, greedy man, a man so selfish and greedy that he'd been willing to torture his own son to get what he wanted.

Alonso spoke, "You refused? Why?"

"Because there is no undoing horror. We must live with the consequences of our choices. But also because he wanted only to relieve himself of his guilt. He did not want to understand, to overcome, to do better. He wanted only peace for himself." Mayuri spoke directly to Jed. "If taking us back would have prevented any of those things, I might have done it. But it would not, not without healing."

"We cannot heal until we remember and reckon," LaKeemba said, and it felt like the air shook around her words.

"The bottle," Jed said. "That's why. Because now, we must remember."

Mayuri stared at Jed. "What bottle?"

"The one that held the world's memories," Jed whispered. "I opened it."

12

After a while, we were all simply holding silence in Sharon's yurt, and LaKeemba reminded us that we had a big day tomorrow, that we all needed our rest. Sharon had given her bed to Mayuri and Lili, so Sharon went with Charlie and Jed to get her set up to sleep on the fold-out sofa in the farmhouse. Alonso walked me back to my yurt.

"You can sleep in my bed if you want," I said, unsure of my invitation but very sure I didn't want to be alone.

"I would like that, Mavis, to have your company on this hard night. But I would not rest with you so near." He leaned down and kissed me softly. "I will be here to see you at first light. We will prepare for the day together."

Alonso turned and walked across the field to his yurt. I put my fingers to my lips—my first kiss, and it was the most perfect thing in those terrible days.

Sleep came hard and didn't stay long. I tossed and turned, trying to get back to sleep, but eventually, I decided just to get up and read. The map rustled when I put on my robe, so instead of picking up my copy of *Mrs. Frisby and the Rats of*

NIMH, a book I loved even on the third reading, I sat down with the map before me.

The map rustled gently in my hands as I laid her out on the table. And that's when I saw them: hundreds of gold dots moving slowly but steadily toward the ocean-blue glow of Charlottesville. More magic people were coming—many more. I felt tears prick my eyes and let out a long sigh.

AT SOME POINT, I must have dozed off while watching that procession of magic because Alonso woke me with a gentle hand on my shoulder. My face was pressed hard into the map, and I knew I must have crease marks on my face. I looked down quickly to see if I had drooled and readied my hand to cover the pool of water. But either I had, for the only time in my life, not drooled while I'd slept, or the map had absorbed it and saved me the embarrassment of having Alonso see it. I whispered a quiet thank you to her as I folded her up and stood.

I could smell coffee, and I scanned the room for the source. I do few things in the morning before passing coffee through my lips, coffee with lots of cream and sugar, and Alonso knew that. He handed me a giant mug with Hermione Granger's face on the side, and he said, "Good morning, sunshine."

I knew what I looked like in the morning—hair flat on one side and standing straight up on the other, puffy eyes, the hitch in my step as my aging hips loosened—but I appreciated the tender smile on his lips. "Good morning, good sir," I said with a slight bow, and his smile broke into a grin. "Thank you for the coffee."

"Meet me outside in ten?"

I gave a brisk nod and took a long sip of the hot coffee before gathering my clothes and jumping into the shower.

When I came outside, the sky was just turning light, and I could hear the birds stirring in the trees along the field where our yurts stood. I didn't see this time of morning often, but when I did, I loved it. It felt like promise, like potential, and we needed all the potential that day might hold.

I took Alonso's hand, and he glanced at me as he gave my fingers a squeeze. It was the first time I'd initiated physical contact, but I needed him to know I felt the same way he did. At least I hoped he felt like I did because it felt good.

We walked down the slope toward the Wilsons' barn, and I expected to see their van parked out front. Instead, there was a school bus, and not one of the old ones that smelled like years of body odor and school books either. Nope, it was one of the new ones. Its paint was still so shiny that it reflected the fading moonlight just a little. The words "Chatham County Public Schools" were painted on the side, and I realized Mrs. Wilson must have worked a little of her magic to get a bus for a non-school venture.

Mr. Wilson was already in the driver's seat, and I was glad that he'd never let his commercial driver's license expire even after almost seventeen years of not driving a big rig up and down the highway. He'd quit and taken to farming when Mrs. Wilson was pregnant with Jed because he wasn't willing to be away from his son even for one night if he could help it.

I was glad Alonso had come to wake me because even with this gentle alarm, we were among the last few to board. I'd drunk most of my coffee on the short walk down, but now I gulped the rest. An open mug of coffee was not a smart idea on a bouncing school bus. The fact that it was new didn't mean it wouldn't send me and my coffee flying if we hit a bump in the road. The knot on my head from when the driver took a hilly mountain road on Jed's field trip to Monticello had been swollen for days.

The ride to Charlottesville from the farm wasn't long, an hour most days, but this early, we would beat even the light traffic down into town. We'd be there in forty-five minutes tops.

Court Square was the part of town where the courthouses for both Charlottesville city and Albemarle County were located. It was also one of the oldest parts of the town. Buildings from the late 1700s were ringing the county courthouse, which had been built in 1803. (Jed had also had a field trip to Court Square last year.) Just up the street was the now-famous statue of Robert E. Lee that white nationalists had gathered around a couple of years earlier after they'd marched through the University of Virginia campus carrying tiki torches and shouting racist things the night before. The statue was still there, surrounded by bright-orange construction fencing as was the one of Stonewall Jackson just outside the courthouse itself.

There was a lot of history in this part of the city. Vinegar Hill, where most of the outdoor walking mall stood just a few blocks from the courthouse, had once been a thriving African American business district before it was demolished to make way for the mostly white mall. The slave auction had taken place there, and until recently, the original auction block had still stood on the property until a local citizen, fed up with the community's failure to address racism, threw the block into the James River. I couldn't say I blamed him.

We were going to this place because the history was thick there. If the voices of those forgotten would be screaming anywhere, it would be there. I was both thrilled and terrified by that fact.

As we came up Vinegar Hill, I began to see people walking toward the Square. A little boy with brown skin and completely white hair was skipping up the sidewalk, and on every third or fourth hop, he'd let himself fly a few feet. A woman with long blonde hair and freckles across her nose was spinning spirals of leaves before her as she walked, and beside her, another woman with dreadlocks and more tattoos than I'd ever seen was chatting with a squirrel on her shoulder. An older white man in a wheelchair seemed to be peeling all the old stickers and tape from the streetlights and buildings as he moved along, a magical street cleaner. The closer to the courthouse we got, the more magical people I saw. The vision made me excited, and it made me feel incredibly nervous, too. There was too much power here, and we were drawing too much attention. This couldn't be good.

"Why are they doing all of that? Right out in the open?" I said to Alonso as I turned to him. I could feel my heart pounding against the back of my throat.

He leaned past me to look out the window.

His smile could have set me at ease, but instead, it made me angry. "Why are you smiling? Poke will surely find us now."

With a sigh and a squeeze of my hand, Alonso sat back. "We want him to find us, Mavis. That's the point. We need to be seen. That's the only way we will get people to pay attention."

Then, he used his chin to gesture toward a small black woman standing at the edge of the sidewalk across from the courthouse. She had her tiny hands out, palms up by her waist, and her lips were moving as if she was repeating something over and over again. "Who is she?"

"That, Mavis, is Amarinta. She is our best defense." Alonso and I kept our eyes on the small woman as we drove by, and I saw a small smile lift the corner of her mouth when she caught our gaze.

"What is her power?" I asked as Mr. Wilson stopped the bus.

"She is our projector. She will let the world know."

"What, like a film projector?" I laughed at the idea.

"Don't laugh, Mavis. Exactly like that. Amarinta is conveying what she sees here to people around the world." He leaned over and kissed my cheek before standing and offering me his hand. "We're here."

As usual, I had so many questions that they were fighting for their space on my tongue, but I finally settled on one as I walked down the tall steps and out of the bus. "She uses the magical ties to share?"

"She does," Alonso said.

I had always been jealous of the not-quite telepathic way magic people talked. Because I had come to my magic differently—it was more of who I am than something I could just do —I had never been privy to that thrum of communication that passed between them. This time, though, I was at the center of the action, so I wasn't going to miss a thing. I wasn't sure I loved that idea.

Mr. Wilson took the bus down the street and turned left in the search for a parking space big enough for the bus. Already the grass around the courthouse was full of people, and while I could feel the buzz of all that magic, I could tell that some of the folks here weren't magical at all. They were spectators, and they had their phones up and recording already. A wave of anxiety brought sweat to my palms.

"Jedidiah's people, come with me." LaKeemba's voice brought, as always, comfort and clarity, and when I looked over at Jed, he was blushing and grinning all at once. He loved that she was calling us his people, and I loved that for him. Plus, she was right. We were all together because of Jedidiah and his power. If he hadn't known that something was stirring that first day, we would have never met one another . . . and I would still be imaginary. I shuddered at the thought.

Our group gathered on the brick front-porch-thing— someone said it was called a portico—of the courthouse. I moved my eyes from face to face, taking peace from my friends. Everyone was there, and that fact settled my soul. We had done amazing things together before. We could do them again.

"It's 8:50. In ten minutes, people around the world will gather just like this, and we will begin to tell our stories. Some of us will speak, and some will listen at first, but eventually, we will all get a chance to share. Our job here is to tell the truth as loudly or as quietly as we feel able."

I swallowed a lump in my throat. I didn't feel very able at all.

"If your magic helps you tell the story, then use it. Fear not. We are strong together. While I cannot make any promises about our safety, we are also safer together. People are guarding us," she looked toward Mr. Wilson, who had just walked up and put his arm around his wife, "and we are watching out for one another, too. Stay together if you can, but if we are separated, meet here in one hour."

Alonso took my hand again, and I took a deep breath. Then, Jed slipped his arm through mine on the other side and said, "I want to listen to you first, Mavis."

I gasped and felt tears burn my eyes. No one had ever before asked to hear my story. I'd shared parts of it with Alonso and Sharon, and of course, Jed had lived most of it. But that he would ask to understand my view on our lives together, that alone made all my fear on this day worth it.

We began to work our way into the crowd. Alonso, Jed, Charlie, and I were together, and I could see that Mr. and Mrs. Wilson were with Sharon, LaKeemba with Lizzie, Lili, and Mayuri. Small huddles of people formed all around us, and then, I heard church bells from somewhere up the street. 9 a.m. Time to begin.

JEDIDIAH

I had never felt so much magic in my life. It felt like I was at a live concert but more intense. The air vibrated with energy, and I could feel it inside my ribs, like a drumbeat.

All around us, people began talking, and the energy got faster, stronger. I looked at Mavis and nodded. She swallowed hard and then said, "The first thing I remember is your tiny hands on the day you came home from the hospital. You grabbed my finger, and I gave you my heart."

I swallowed hard so that I concentrated on what Mavis was saying. I didn't want to cry, but I knew it was more important that I really hear Mavis than that I try to look tough or something.

She went on to tell us about how she'd loved being my friend alone when I was little because she got to spend all her time with me. We played games and told each other stories, and at night, she'd watch me sleep.

I remembered some of that, like the twenty billion games of Candy Land, but the rest felt far away. I recognized what she was saying, but I didn't remember much, not from back when I was little. Mostly I could remember hanging out with Mavis when I got home from school. She talked about that, too. I guess she was really proud of me when I popped my first wheelie and when I learned I could help people carry their secrets around.

She talked up to today and said that when she'd become unimaginary, it had been the scariest and most wonderful thing. She loved being seen, and when she said that part, she looked at Alonso. "I think you, after Jed, were the one to really see me first."

He bent down and took her hand and kissed it.

Charlie looked at me and rolled his eyes, but he was smiling.

"The thing is," she said, "things are still great. Just different, I guess. And now, I have this map, and it feels like a real responsibility. A good one, but heavy, you know?"

Charlie, Alonso, and I nodded. We did know. All of us. Maybe that's what I was feeling in the air—all that responsibility bouncing around among us. I squeezed Mavis's hand.

She smiled at me. "Thank you, Jed."

I smiled back and then leaned over and kissed her cheek. I'd never done that before, but it felt like the right thing, the right new thing for who we were as friends now.

When I stepped back, she put her fingers to her cheek and wiped a tear away before smiling at me again.

13

I'd watched Jed's face as I talked because I didn't want to hurt him. I didn't want him to feel like he was responsible for my loneliness, my sadness, my fear, but Jed was smart. He didn't feel like those things were his fault; I could tell. And when he kissed me on the cheek, all grown up, I realized I didn't have to feel responsible for those things of his either. He heard me, he knew, and he still loved me. It was amazing.

Alonso cleared his throat and said, "My turn?"

The three of us nodded, and I braced myself. I hadn't heard much of Alonso's story yet. He wasn't secretive, not really. He just didn't talk much at all and much less about himself.

"I was born in North Carolina in 1930. My parents were tobacco sharecroppers, and my brother and sisters and I all worked the fields with them after school." His voice was solid, but his eyes had gone soft, like he had slid back in time.

"One day, my daddy lost two fingers in the tobacco picker, and while he was okay, mostly, it meant he couldn't work the machine very well. I was nine, but I started to run the machine for us."

"You were running a picker at nine?" Jed asked.

Some of our neighbors grew tobacco, so we all knew what those machines looked like. No one would dare let a child work one of them now.

Charlie frowned at Jed sideways. "Is that odd?"

"It is now," I said, "but I expect back then, it was just normal, huh?"

Alonso nodded. "Daddy had tried to keep us away from the machine because of how dangerous it was. But a lot of kids ran equipment then, same as back in your time, Charlie. But I wasn't big enough yet, couldn't get the plants into the machine very well on my own, so my sister Bess helped."

He swallowed hard, and I felt myself brace.

"She slipped one day, slid down into the machine, and my brother and I couldn't get her out in time." Alonso ran a hand down his face. "Mom made us stop farming after that. We moved into town, and Daddy took a job at a soda counter. He wasn't ever quite the same after. Quieter. More to himself."

I squeezed his hand, and he continued. "But it was about then that I knew I could do something other people couldn't. I was sweeping the sidewalk in front of the drugstore where Daddy worked. He'd gotten me a job there so I could earn a little more for the family. A woman walked by."

All around us, I could hear people talking, a murmur behind Alonso's words. On the edges of sound, though, I could hear screams. The Unremembered were coming. I took a deep breath and forced myself to pay close attention to Alonso.

"This woman was working some kind of magic, a peace weaving, maybe. I didn't know enough about the things people could do with magic to really understand, but I felt this impulse —so strong and clear in myself. So I reached out and touched her when she stopped at the corner."

The screams were getting louder, and I braced, both for their entrance but also for the next moment in Alonso's story.

"Immediately, I felt my strength pass to her, and I felt her magic get bigger somehow. She must have felt it too because she didn't immediately jerk away." He paused and took a long, slow breath. "She looked down at my hand and then into my face. I think she almost smiled, but then a sneer replaced the smile as she screamed, 'Nigger, don't touch me,' and smacked me across the cheek."

I gasped and pulled Alonso's hand to my chest. "What happened?"

The sorrow on his face carved deep lines around his mouth. "People heard her, of course, and if I had been a little older, it would have gone terribly wrong for me then. But because I was a little boy, my daddy took the brunt of it. He got a fierce beating to teach him that he needed to 'learn his boy' better about his place." Tears sat pooled in Alonso's eyes. "The learning took, of course. It took me a long time to touch a white person again." He looked down at our hands and let the tears fall.

I pulled his hand to my lips and then looked at Jed and Charlie. Both of them were still as tree stumps. They had heard every word, and in our small circle, a light grew brighter. I'd noticed it when I was telling my story, like the sun had started to move out from behind a cloud, but it was subtle then. Now, it looked like the sun had burned the cloud away.

The screams of the Unremembered were getting even louder, and at the edge of my vision, I could see something dark gathered in the alley beside the Swan Tavern across the street. I took a deep breath and turned to look at it directly. There, with a swarm of screams gathered around it, was The Shadow, and this time, it had attached itself to Poke.

I turned to Charlie, and he was staring right at his father. For a second, I thought he was going to run—toward his father or away, I wasn't sure—but then, he raised his hand.

"Charlie, no," Jed shouted, and I knew that we both feared the same thing—Charlie was going to use his power to stop time and freeze us all here. LaKeemba had warned us on the way over: once this process of remembering started, it couldn't stop for any reason or all the power would collapse into darkness again, making the Unremembered and their malignant leader, who was taking advantage of their pain, even more powerful.

Charlie glanced at Jed, smiled, and then waved at his dad. "You all know my story," he said without breaking eye contact with his father. "You don't know his though. I think it's time."

I looked from Charlie back to Poke, and I saw Poke shaking his head. He couldn't have possibly heard what his son had said, but still, Poke was trying to warn him off. The Shadow stepped out into the street and furled out to fill the block.

"When he was growing up, my daddy's best friend was a little slave boy named Peter. The two of them were always together, doing chores and making mischief. Peter's mama was the cook, and so both boys wandered through the kitchen all hours of the day. Daddy told me that his favorite thing was when Peter's mama would make biscuits and then let them push a finger into the hot bread before she filled the hole with molasses."

Alonso pulled my hand to his stomach and held it tight with both of his. I prepared myself for what was coming. This was a story I knew would not end well. I had heard enough about slave times to know that.

"One day, Granddaddy Lester came in while Daddy and Peter were eating biscuits on the floor of the kitchen. He'd seen them do that a dozen times before, but that day, he was mad, striking mad because his girl," Charlie winced at the words, "Matilda, Peter's sister, had run away."

I knew what it meant for Matilda to be Lester's girl, and I would have run away too if I was supposed to just let somebody attack me like that all the time.

"Because he was so mad, Grandaddy picked Peter up by the shirt and hauled him to the stocks."

I gritted my teeth, remembering how Charlie had been put in those same stocks by his father. The legacy of violence was loud and clear.

"The next day, Peter was gone, sold down South." Charlie's voice was so quiet now that I had to lean in to hear what he said next. "That broke something in Daddy, something that probably would have gotten broken someday anyway, but it broke him early, losing his best friend like that. He never let himself be soft again. Not ever."

I imagined Poke as a tiny boy with bright-red hair and molasses all over his hands and face, watching his friend get pulled away for doing nothing other than being a little boy. I might have gotten hard, too, especially if I didn't have friends to remind me of my tenderness. Slavery just sucked all the tenderness out of most people though. I'd been around people held by it long enough to know that. The folks who came out tender—black folks or white folks—were rare.

Charlie had never broken his stare with his dad, and now I could see that the man was almost to us. He was pushing his way through the crowd, and in just a few more steps, he'd be at our circle. I turned to face him with Alonso, and I saw Jed reach out to put his hand on Charlie's shoulder.

"Hi, Daddy. I want you to know. I forgive you." Charlie's voice chimed through the air like church bells.

14

I watched Poke's eyes widen, so I knew he had heard Charlie. For a second, I thought I saw his face soften, but then, quick as a blink, his jaw set, and he and The Shadow took a step forward with the Unremembered coming right behind them.

I groaned. It felt, in that moment, that kindness and love could never win, but then Alonso squeezed my hand, and Jed winked at me. Then I remembered. We'd won with love and kindness before, and I knew we would again. How I was sure, I couldn't say, and that realization sent my stomach rocketing to my knees, but I was certain.

And I knew what I had to do. I had to feel sympathy for that little boy that Poke was. I had to set my heart to love, as Sharon said, and push my way forward with it. I couldn't think about what Poke had done to my friends or me, what he had done to his son. There would be time enough later for justice and consequences. Now, though, in the thick of it, I had to grab hold of love tight and surge forth.

I heard LaKeemba's voice echo among the buildings, "Now. Listen."

Like a bowl had dropped over all of us gathered there in Court Square, silence descended. It wasn't that sound disappeared. I could still hear the shifting of bodies all around, and the bracelets on Shelby's wrist jangled gently in the air. No, our desire to be heard, to be noted, it fell away, and we all turned toward the screams of the Unremembered.

At first, the howls were painful, almost too much for me to bear. They felt like they were clawing their way through my eardrums. But then, I chose one voice, a woman's voice that reached me in some sharp, particular way, and I bore my listening down on her words.

"He left. He left me, just like I had always feared he would. He left me alone in our new house, hundreds of miles away from everyone I knew. He took our only car and left. He left me with the flu, sobbing on the floor. He left me."

As I listened, her words turned from screams into sobs, and soon, all I could hear were her gasps for breath and then a quiet sniffling.

I leaned in and looked, seeking her face amongst the shadows, and there, at the edge of the gathered shadows, I saw the features of a young woman turn toward me. Tears ran tunnels down her face, but she was looking at me, gazing at me in fact.

I nodded my head. "Oh, I'm so sorry. That was awful. So awful," I whispered. "What a terrible thing to have lived through. I'm sorry he did that to you. I'm sorry you were so alone." My words welled up from my heart, and I let them pour out as I told her all the things I could think of to let her know I heard her, that I understood as best I could. I wanted her to know she was not alone.

She kept staring at me, and her breaths slowed down. Then, a smile turned up one corner of her mouth. Not a smile of happiness. It was the kind of smile you give someone who has done a kindness for you, even if you still don't feel happy. It was gratitude in flesh.

I blinked, and the next minute she was gone. I scoured the gray figures at the back of The Shadow, but she was nowhere to be found.

I didn't have much time to wonder about that, though, because I then heard a little boy's shouts. "Help me. Help me. I'm down here."

I listened until I found his small face, and in time, he saw me and told me about how he'd fallen down a cliff, how he'd been able to hear people looking for him but unable to shout loudly enough for them to find him. Eventually, he too disappeared after I told him, "I see you. I found you."

The gray mass was growing lighter, and I could see beams of sunlight reaching the ground amongst the figures. I turned to my sides and saw my friends and others leaning forward. Their eyes were locked on the figures, and I knew they were listening.

I heard the words of a young gay man who was kicked out by his family and then an older woman whose children never came to visit her in the nursing home. I heard a little boy sobbing because the bullies had beat him up again and his dad said he needed to just toughen up. I kept listening, kept hearing, and with each story, the day grew lighter until, finally, all the gray figures were gone, and it was only The Shadow towering over Poke.

Then, LaKeemba's voice sounded over the crowd again. "Retreat, friends. We will take on this battle another way." I took a deep breath and felt the weariness in my shoulders like someone had laid a boulder on each side of my head. I stumbled backwards with everyone else.

Eventually, I turned my back on The Shadow, too. I wasn't sure what it would do if we looked away, but I couldn't keep walking backwards, not with steps and statues behind me. LaKeemba had her back squarely toward it as she walked a few steps in front of me, so I figured it was alright.

And when I looked back, it and Poke were gone. The patch of grass where they'd been standing was flooded with sunlight.

WE ALL MADE our way silently to our vehicles, giving small waves and tiny smiles as we headed back to where we had come from. On our bus, the silence was comforting. I settled into my seat and rested my head against the window. With each bump, my head bounced against the glass a bit, just hard enough to remind me where I was but not hard enough to hurt. Eventually, I must have fallen asleep because the next thing I knew, we were turning onto the farm lane, and everyone was starting to shuffle as they gathered their things.

Alonso picked up the backpack I used as a quasi-purse, and we made our way off the bus and to my yurt. He kissed me on the cheek and squeezed my hand before turning to head home without a word. I was grateful for his presence and his quiet. I'd had enough words for just then.

I spent that afternoon cross-stitching at the dining room table. I had been working on a scene of a cat in a sewing room for months now, and I usually only managed to get a few dozen stitches done while I watched TV at night. Today, though, I sewed for hours and let the concentration required to pull threads and count stitches soothe me.

While I sewed, I remembered a week when Jed was about eight. His parents had taken a trip to China, where Mr. Wilson was giving goat-raising advice to farmers as part of a cultural exchange program. Jed's grandmother had come to stay with him, and while she was a kind woman, Jed really missed his parents.

So after school, he and I perched ourselves on a big pile of dirt at the back of the barn and made it our job to sort all the rocks out. I have no idea whether this task was something that actually needed to be done or just something that Jed came on as a way of staying busy . . . but it worked. He and I dug holes with our hands and made a huge pile of stones. We talked a little, but mostly, we dug and tossed rocks, and somehow, it made both of us feel better. When the Wilsons came home, they built a wall from those rocks, and every time I saw it, I remembered the peace I felt in that simple task of digging and piling. Cross-stitch made me feel the same way. I hoped Jed had something like this to do, too.

As the sun began to set, I stood up and stretched. Then, I heard my stomach. I hadn't eaten since breakfast, and I was starving. When I stepped out the door of my yurt onto the stoop, I smelled the most amazing scent. Wood smoke and pork, and I headed right for the firepit.

Sure enough, Mr. Wilson was there with pork shoulder on a spit. He was turning the handle around and around, and I wondered if this was like cross-stitching or digging out rocks for him. When he saw me, he smiled and pointed toward a camp chair next to him. "Keep me company?" he said.

I smiled and sat down. "Smells amazing. How long have you been out here?"

He set the handle of the spit in a metal loop at the edge of the fire and dropped into another chair. "A few hours. I figured we'd all be hungry soon, and while I can't do magic, I can help."

I looked at him closely then, and for the first time, I noticed the dark shadows under his eyes. "You are more than just a help, Mr. Wilson. I think we all need you because you are a rock."

He shook his head a little.

"No, seriously. You keep us all grounded, tied down when the magic makes it seem like we can float away." I felt tears prick my eyes because I realized that what I was saying was true. "Today, it gave me great comfort to see you at the wheel of that bus and to know that while this is hard on you, too, you would get us home safely, no matter what."

A small smile passed his lips, and he tugged on his chin. "Thank you, Mavis." He reached into a cooler beside him and took out two bottles of lemonade, passing one to me.

I leaned back and let my head drop over the back of the chair. Above me, the stars were just beginning to come out, and I watched them twinkle as they appeared. They were so small from here, but I knew that if I were standing next to them, they'd burn me up. I knew there was some metaphor in that somewhere, but tonight, I was just too tired to figure it out.

Mr. Wilson and I sat there for a while longer, just the two of us, letting the fire dance and the pork cook. Every few minutes, one of us would turn the spit and then sit back down. It was peaceful, perfect almost.

Soon, other folks starting joining us. Jed, Charlie, and Mrs. Wilson came first, then Sharon with Shelby. Alonso and LaKeemba next, and soon the rest of the folks from our encampment came out. In the course of a few minutes, everyone had tea or lemonade, and Mr. Wilson took the pork off the spit and cut it up on a folding table that Charlie and Jed had brought out from the barn. Mrs. Wilson and Sharon went into the farmhouse and came back with a huge bowl of coleslaw and rolls.

The BBQ sandwiches, dressed with Mr. Wilson's famous hot pepper vinegar, were perfect. Messy and filling and just hot enough to burn your lips when you took a bite. I'm not sure I'd ever tasted anything so good.

As we tucked the dirty paper plates and used bottles into a trash bag, Sharon began to sing.

When peace like a river descendeth my way
And sorrows like sea billows roll,
Whatever the cost, I have learned how to say,
It is well. It is well with my soul.

. . .

By some unspoken understanding, we knew Sharon's rich voice signaled the end of our evening, and we all wandered, silent again, to our beds. I slept, without dreams, until the first rays of the sun woke me. It was blissful . . . and that bliss would carry me far into the next day's horrors.

JEDIDIAH

I knew that song Sharon sang from church, and when Mom was stressed, she sang it, too. She had told me that, when she was pregnant with me, she sang it to me every day while she took a shower. "It comforted me, Jed, and I hoped it would comfort you."

And it did. Every time I heard it, I felt calmer, more focused maybe. Safer. So that night, when Charlie and I got into bed, I slept well for the first time in a long time. I didn't dream about Poke or The Shadow like I had for the past few nights, and when I woke up, I felt good. For a little while.

Mom and Dad were already out by the firepit, cooking eggs and bacon over the flame. That was one of Dad's favorite things. He loved to cook over a fire. He wasn't one of those stereotypical dudes who didn't think men should cook, and he did make dinner sometimes. Mostly, though, Mom cooked in the kitchen. But outside, Dad ruled the fire.

He had this huge cast-iron griddle that weighed about a billion pounds, and he'd set it up on a stand so it sat just above the flame. There, he had one side full of strips of bacon from the pigs at the farm up the street, and our hens' eggs were scrambled and cooking on the other side. I felt my mouth begin to water as I sat down on a log next to Mom.

She handed me my favorite drink for campfires—half hot cocoa, one-quarter milk, and one-quarter coffee. Too much coffee made me jittery, but I loved the taste of it, especially mixed with hot cocoa. I took a long sip and then pulled back my chin and looked at her, "Is that cinnamon?"

She winked. "Like it?"

I took another sip. "Actually, yeah. It's really good."

She smiled and held out a plate while Dad piled up the bacon.

Soon, everyone else gathered by the fire and started serving themselves while Dad filled the griddle again. People were teasing each other about hoarding the bacon, and it felt good, good to be with everybody, good to laugh.

But then, I felt it. There, out by the end of the lane, The Shadow was coming.

I tried to look casual as I stood up and walked around like I wanted to stretch my legs. I strolled toward the rise in the pasture that gave me a better look at the road. I looked back and saw LaKeemba following me. She was moving slowly, and I assumed she was trying to seem laid-back, too. People wouldn't buy it for long, though.

I slowed my pace a bit and let her catch up, and then I told her, "It's here."

"Yeah, I feel it, too. Not like you, but a little, like a tremor in a spider's web."

I looked at her. "Wouldn't we be the ones making the tremor though, like a trapped insect? And it's the spider?"

"That's what we hope it thinks." She smiled wryly and quickened her pace.

When we reached the end of the lane, I could see it there, a black mass spanning from the driveway across the front of the empty farmhouse across the street. It was bigger now, darker, too, and Poke was right in the midst of it. Other people milled around inside The

Shadow. I couldn't make out any faces, but if they were in the thrall of that thing, then they were dangerous, even if what was making them follow that thing was just fear or hurt.

LaKeemba and I stood still, just watching. I was even afraid to eat a piece of bacon for fear the crunch of it would draw attention. But I needn't have worried. The Shadow wasn't interested in us, not yet. If LaKeemba were right, it didn't know it was caught in our web, but I didn't really want to wait until it realized it was trapped . . . and besides, I didn't know what our trap was yet, and I figured it was about time to figure it out.

Silently, LaKeemba put her arm around my shoulders and turned us back toward the fire. "It's time," was all she said.

15

———

I hadn't even noticed Jed and LaKeemba were gone, but as they strode back into camp, I could tell something was up. They walked like they meant business, and as they returned to the fire, all of us grew quiet. Mr. Wilson used thick welding gloves to lift the griddle off its stand and lean it against the stones of the firepit. Then, he lifted the spit and stirred the logs with his poker.

"Make it roar, Alan. Even higher than we talked about," LaKeemba said.

I looked at Jed, and his brow furrowed. Apparently, neither of us knew that his dad and LaKeemba had already talked.

"They are here, friends," LaKeemba said, and I could hear her voice echo through the woods at the back of the pasture. "We are ready."

I wanted to object, to say that I had no idea what was happening and, thus, could not be ready, but something in the way LaKeemba stood told me that I was wrong about that.

"We were given that bottle, given a map, and given our powers for a reason. 'For such a time as this,' Queen Esther said. We now do what we were made and then prepared to do."

I felt the map rustle in my pocket, and when I pulled it out, I saw the gold dots converging again. This time, they were coming here. For the first time, I understood what all those books meant when people said their hearts swelled with hope. Mine felt like it was about four times larger than usual. For a moment, I imagined that if I didn't keep my feet purposefully on the ground, I might just rise, chest first, into the air. That's how glad I was to see all those glowing spots gathering.

And when I looked up, people were walking toward the fire from every direction, even from the road where The Shadow and Poke were lurking. Dozens of people then hundreds, all converging on our farm. I had never been privy to how the telepathy of magic people worked, but I was so glad it did.

Soon, more than five hundred people spread out across the pasture, and I had a sudden wash of worry. How could all these people hear LaKeemba? But almost as soon as I had the thought, I realized that they didn't need to hear her if they just knew what she was thinking. Then, all that hope deflated in my chest. I couldn't hear that way, so I would be left out. Again. Alone, even in a crowd of people.

I looked around and then down at my map. I was there, too. I knew I was, but at that moment, it didn't feel like it. For a second, I thought about slipping away, going to my yurt, and staying there until it was all over. But then I looked at all the people there, all the people taking not only the risk to come to this place but to take action, and my self-pity faded away. My hurt feelings didn't matter. We had something to do, and I would figure out a way to help, even if I couldn't know what everyone else knew.

Now, I'd be lying if I pretended like I wasn't terrified. I was beyond terrified. We had to fight that awful thing across the road—that alone had me sweaty with fear. But now I had to find a way to help without help. My hands started to shake.

Just then, though, it felt like something fell away from my

ears, and I thought of that story in the Bible where Saul who becomes Paul is healed by that old guy. The phrase is something like "the scales fell away," and it felt the same for me except maybe it was that gauze had fallen out of my ears because now, out of nowhere, I could hear all the magic people. Well, not really hear them, not like they were talking, but I could feel them in me, feel what they were doing, what they were feeling.

I had imagined what this experience would be like many times. When I could tell Jed and Alonso were communicating something I couldn't catch, or that Sharon and Mrs. Wilson were connected in a way that I wasn't part of, I had pretended I felt what they did, and sometimes, just the idea of it felt overwhelming.

But now, it wasn't, not even with all these people here, connected to me. It didn't feel overwhelming at all. It felt, and I felt silly for even thinking of it, but it's the best word—it felt empowering, like someone had taken who I was at the very center of myself and supercharged me. It felt like nights at the Wilsons' dinner table when we all laughed at old jokes and told stories about our days. It felt like the times we'd fought The Shadow before. It felt like nights when Jed was little and sleeping with his head in my lap. It felt like all the best things, the things that let me be me.

I reveled in the feeling for a minute, and then I let it settle into me, and I listened, or felt, or . . . I can't really describe it at all. I just knew, right then, that all I needed to do was do what I could, what only I could do the way I could do it. So I waited for the moment, the moment I knew, somehow, was coming, and I watched.

Around me, everyone else had stilled. We were all facing the road now, and I could see us—people of all shapes and sizes, all skin colors and genders, all manner of piercings and tattoos (we were a people who liked our body art, apparently, because there were a lot of piercings and tattoos)—waiting, together, for the right moment. It felt like that childhood song but real. "Red and yellow, black and white, they are precious in His sight," except that I winced a little at the red and yellow parts. No Native American or Asian people refer to themselves that way, and it made me feel icky.

I felt a hand slip into mine, and I looked over to see Alonso beside me. I stretched up and kissed his cheek. Then, a hand touched the small of my back, and Mrs. Wilson stepped up on my other side with Jed, Charlie, and Mr. Wilson as well. LaKeemba, Sharon, and Shelby lined up next to Alonso, and then, as one, we took a single step forward.

JEDIDIAH

I'm not sure why I started, but as we walked forward, I began to draw in the air again. I remembered the times I'd done it before, how much power I felt rushing through me. I felt like I was doing something I was simply made to do, and it was amazing.

Above my head, I trailed sketches of people, people I knew somehow from all over the world. All of us were walking. Some of us were moving our arms, some staring straight ahead. All of us, magic, though, and all of us working that magic big and strong as we moved forward.

Ahead of us, beyond where my hands kept drawing, I saw The Shadow, or what I now realized was our fragment of The Shadow, moving forward. Fast. I drew faster and faster, casting lines and faces into the air so that everyone around me could see them. I had no idea how this would help us here, in this final battle—and this would be the final battle, I knew—but I knew it was what I was supposed to do.

I had first seen this shadow when I was just a little boy, and it had terrified me. But even then, I had stood up to it. Now, I was standing up again, with all my friends beside me, and I felt powerful. Powerful and scared.

16

Jed was the first of us to begin working his magic, but once his hands were in the drawing, we were on it. I saw Shelby turn her hands upward, as she did when she was receiving a great vision, and Mrs. Wilson walked over to wrap an arm around her waist, our two prophets seeking wisdom. Alonso reached over and put his hand on LaKeemba's arm as she stretched her body wide and back in an arc, spelling protection over all of us. Lizzie turned into her shadow self, and even Charlie, whose ability to stop time was sometimes too blunt a force for most moments, had managed to hold back the traffic on the road in front of the farm by freezing the area around us.

I took a deep breath, squeezed Alonso's hand, and went invisible. I had never loved when I had to stay invisible without a choice, but now that I could do it at will—it was thrilling. I gave Alonso's fingers another squeeze, felt his answering pressure, and then let go. I didn't know exactly what I needed to do, but I knew I needed to move.

I slipped back in the crowd gathered in the hayfield in front of the barn and saw Marcus, a friend who must have returned with the gathering crowd, corralling the goats into their room at the back while also coaching the chickens into their coop. I was grateful that the animals weren't needed in the battle and even more grateful that Marcus's gift of communicating with them meant they would be safe. I gave him a nod, only to realize too late that he couldn't see me. Still, he looked near where I was and said, "Good on you, Mavis."

I smiled. The magic people network was working just fine, even with me as part of it, and I shivered with delight . . . until I saw The Shadow flowing down the lane past the garden and up to the porch of the farmhouse. Then the shivers transformed into terror.

Still, the sight of all of us, all of us magic people working together, gave me courage. By the garden on the other side of the farmhouse from the barn, a group of women was circled up, and I could see the tendrils of the pea plants and the tiny shoots of the marigold stems growing and stretching, reaching out to Poke and The Shadow with their green lives. As each plant reached the darkness, it burst into light before burning to the ground, and for a minute, The Shadow grew fainter, less opaque.

Beyond the garden women in the cow pasture, a single man with the skin the color of ivory stood, his arms out beside him, palms forward. Around him, our neighbor's cattle were lowing and forming an arc of bovine strength. At his word, they charged forward, knocking down the fence and charging straight into The Shadow. Poke had only a split second to jump out of the way before a huge bull barreled right into the belly of the darkness. The animal's bellow sounded like a horn of triumph as he emerged from the other side, unscathed. Where the bull had emerged, The Shadow was thinner, and I could see tiny shafts of light beginning to shine through The Shadow's fog-like body.

I kept moving as I watched everyone else work. I skirted the flattened pasture fence and charged up the pasture, paralleling the driveway. Only then did I realize what I was doing—I was flanking The Shadow and its people.

Jed had never really been one of those young boys who liked war books or playing soldier, but for a couple of years, he had read everything he could find—and that his parents would let him read—on battle maneuvers in the Civil War. Someone had come by one day and asked if they could metal detect in the Wilsons' pasture because they said a Confederate Army hospital had been there. The Wilsons had declined that request, but just the idea of soldiers having been on his lands had set him to learning everything he could about the movements of the Union and Confederate armies in the area. He'd even made us all go to the Chancellorsville Battlefield so we could see where Confederate General Stonewall Jackson had led a successful flank attack on the Union Army.

To his credit, Jed never rooted for the Confederates, and when we went to Chancellorsville, he started to cry. "If the Union had only been paying attention, the war might have ended soon. Slavery might have ended sooner," he said as he looked at the battlefield where more than eleven thousand men died. Then, he'd walked to the car and never studied war again.

Now, though, I was grateful to see that The Shadow, Poke, and their people hadn't protected their flank either. As I came up beside where the crowd of The Shadow's followers gathered along the driveway to the farm, no one even glanced my way. I was invisible, of course, but since some of those people had magic, they'd have noticed me if they'd been paying even the least bit of attention.

I slid quickly behind a clump of cedar trees just beyond the Wilsons' greenhouse and let myself be visible again. Then, I closed my eyes and sent out the signal. I pictured it like I was flashing the bat signal in the air, a giant beam of light that said, "Here, we can reach him here."

In all the previous times I had run into The Shadow, and as far as I could tell from what anyone else had shared, none of us had gotten close enough to see inside the monster. But now, from where I stood, I could see. Right in the middle of that deep darkness was a well of even more intense darkness. There, I could see its heart, and it was like looking into a cave without an end.

We needed to shine a light there, and we needed as many of us as possible to do it. I was rallying the troops, and the troops were rallying. All around me, people turned toward The Shadow and worked their magic toward it. Across the farm lane at the edge of the hayfield, I could see Jed drawing with wider and wider swings of his arms, and his face was set, his eyes shining. I couldn't see what he was drawing, but it was vast, bigger than anything I'd ever seen him construct before. In the few seconds I was watching, I saw his face break into a smile, and I grounded my hope in what he saw, even when I couldn't.

A tiny body pressed up against my legs, and I looked down to see Lili. She rested her cheek against my thigh, and then she held out her hands, just like I'd seen her do in that video, and the air around me got thicker as she pushed toward Poke. She was holding him and The Shadow away and keeping their backs to me. I smiled down at her and pushed my signal farther into the edges of the farm, as far as I could envision the roads and the land.

Mayuri slid up beside her daughter, and when she met my eyes, she gave the briefest nod, and then she began. She tilted her head back, and I saw her draw in a deep breath. Then, she pursed her lips and whistled. The tune was beautiful, not exactly happy, but not sad either. It was the kind of song that was made for whistling. It reminded me of old stories about rambling gardens and the scene of roses, and it drew me in, helped me feel safe.

It drew others, too, because out of the air around us, people began to emerge. They were dressed in the clothes of history: high collars or long robes, corsets and top hats, sandals and turbans, and their skin color ranged from almost black to the palest, palest cream. An older woman with a bindi on her forehead bent and kissed Lili's head before she turned toward me, nodded, and began weaving light from the sunbeams around us. She spun the rays into a ball, and she sent it sailing on the breeze right into the middle of The Shadow. For a minute, I saw the creature shudder and start to turn, but Lili braced herself between her mother and me and held it where it stood, its raw back to us.

All around, the people that Mayuri called forth from across time gathered here, even as those close to us answered my call. We were all coming here to fight The Shadow.

I glanced down at the map that I had spread between my feet on the ground and was surprised to see similar gatherings of gold orbs all over the world. It was only then that I realized The Shadow was not one but one in many, and it was everywhere. And everywhere it was, magic people were fighting, together . . . where some of us struck a blow against its menace, all of us would find hope.

Back near the farmhouse, I saw a man with long black hair spinning the wind into small tornadoes and sending them one after another into The Shadow. Over by the barn, a young boy was sculpting what looked like a centaur from the muddy path created by the tractor. In moments, the animal came to life and charged at The Shadow, and Poke had only a split second to jump out of the way for the second time.

Then, Poke saw me, and he screamed with a rage so loud that it battered my chest, even over the sound of the battle around me. I felt Lili falter against me, and then, The Shadow turned.

My breath caught in my throat as the creature's not-face looked at me, and I wanted to scream. I wanted to run. But instead, I put my hand on the back of Lili's head, felt Mayuri's fingers grip mine, and I shouted with everything I had, "NOW!"

I felt the force of my word echo across the farm and beyond, and when I looked down at the map, I saw the paper flutter, too. I had sounded the battle cry, and it had been heard.

17

────────

A few times, I had helped Mr. Wilson bail hay. I'd ride along on the trailer and help lift the bails to the center after he tossed them up. Each time after a couple of hours, I had felt like my arms were going to give out, that I might fall over if I had to lift even one more bail. But then, I'd look and see we only had a few more to go, and I'd find more strength to finish. The sight of the end brought forth the last strength buried deep within me.

Now, as I watched the people around me draw deep from their magic, I could see the end. The Shadow was so thin that I could almost make out the columns of the farmhouse porch. But there was still a gray to the air, like smoke from last night's fire was lingering around us. All we had to do was dissipate that smoke, and then, then we would be done.

On one side of the farmhouse porch, I could see LaKeemba and Alonso. They were still standing tall, but sweat gleamed on their faces. Their protection was still in place, but they were coming close to the end of their strength. We need to finish this now.

From across the lane, I caught Jed's eye, and he nodded with one crisp drop of his chin. Then, his left hand flung far into the air, and he drew with one wide arc, a rainbow. An older Asian woman behind him caught the rainbow in the prism of color she had carved from the sunshine around her, and a tiny man with skin the color of worn leather curved that rainbow right into the heart of The Shadow.

From my side of the farm lane, the women working the garden plants shoved a wide rope of pea shoots in to meet the rainbow from our side, and all around, all the magic of all the people gathered focused on The Shadow. I braced for an explosion, but rather than blast apart, The Shadow just evaporated, like fog under the morning sun. It was the most understated and most beautiful thing I'd ever seen. We had won, and no one had been hurt.

Well, almost no one. Poke and the people who had huddled at The Shadow's heart weren't physically hurt. No blood or broken bones, but they were certainly scarred. As the light of day reached them, they shielded their eyes and cowered, and I thought of all the movies where people come out of caves or basements where they'd been trapped for a long time and smiled.

The people from The Shadow didn't turn to us with love, though. They weren't grateful for the rescue. No, they were full of rage, and they were headed for us.

I looked around for an escape route, a way for all of us to get out of these angry people's way, but so many of us were there, all spread across the farm, that at least some of us would be in danger. I looked again at Poke and the people around him and thought of the stories I'd read of lynch mobs that sought out someone they thought had done them wrong. These folks didn't have pitchforks or torches, but from the looks of hate on their faces, they didn't need them.

I was still looking for a way out and feeling helpless when Mohindor appeared in the middle of the group next to Poke. He looked over his shoulder at LaKeemba behind him, and she nodded. Then, he swung his robe wide and took every one of those people away.

I gasped at the suddenness of it all and looked wide-eyed at LaKeemba, who was now walking toward me down the farm lane. "It's okay, Mavis. They are safe. Just in a place where they cannot do harm for now. They need to recover, find their way anew."

As she spoke, Mohindor appeared beside her. "Done," he said quietly.

"Thank you," LaKeemba said. "You are alright?"

"I am fine. I may look a little slow," he winked at me, "but I move quick as lightning."

"Where did you take them?" I asked, but I regretted almost immediately the question because I wasn't sure I wanted to know. I didn't want to think about Poke and all the other folks who had given that thing its power, and I didn't want to hear something terrible.

Mohindor put an arm around my shoulder and led me toward the fire as LaKeemba walked beside us.

"You had a plan for this?" I said, looking from him to her and back again.

LaKeemba smiled. "You know I always have a plan."

"We knew of a place, a place some of us have long used as a retreat of sorts," Mohindor said.

For a second, I imagined a spa with massages and facials and wondered why we would send people who had wanted to kill us to a place to relax. I frowned.

Mohindor's laugh startled me. "No, not that kind of retreat, Mavis. They are on an island that human life has not yet touched. They have food and water, shelter, too. But they can harm no one but themselves." He reached out and touched my hand. "Even then, the labor involved to form weapons may be more than they are willing to undertake, and they definitely won't be getting mani-pedis." He winked at me again.

I imagined Poke trying to carve a spear from some tropical tree on a sandy beach, and the image I got of a red-headed Tom Hanks with a volleyball for a best friend sent me laughing so hard that I fell to the ground and rolled.

Soon, Jed was sitting beside me, and he was laughing, too. I couldn't tell you what he thought was funny, but the two of us kept the hysteria going for so long that Alonso eventually pulled me up by the arms and helped me to the fire, but I still giggled every time I looked at Jed.

While we walked, I heard LaKeemba explain to Charlie where his dad and the others had gone, and he nodded. I couldn't read his face, but I thought there was some relief there amongst the sadness.

Everyone who had gathered at the farm soon convened in the pasture. Mr. Wilson stoked the big fire, and around the hayfield, smaller fires appeared in rings of stone that had magically appeared. Soon, everyone was seated quietly, resting, talking softly, honoring what had just happened.

Alonso took my hand as he sat next to me in a camp chair by our fire, and I leaned over to kiss his cheek. I was so grateful to be near him again and so grateful he and LaKeemba had been strong enough to ward off The Shadow's attack while we fought it. I thought about how it just evaporated like mist, and I looked at LaKeemba. "It's not dead, is it?"

She shook her head as she stared into the fire. "No. The Shadow is not something that can be killed, not by humans, anyway. No, it's just gone from now, forced to leave, but it will find new people who thrive in its fear. We will not, I think, have to fight it again, though. It will not test our light in this life further."

I sighed and nodded. That last part, the part about us not having to fight again, that sounded good. Still, I would not wish this battle on anyone, even though I was glad we wouldn't have to fight it again.

As dusk began to settle around the farm, I leaned my head back and stared at the sky. Jed had drawn a rainbow, and together, we had pushed light into the darkness. I thought of the old Bible story of Noah and the Ark, about how God had sent a rainbow as a promise that God would never again destroy the earth by water. I'd always loved that story and the symbol of it. But now I thought of it differently. God had not promised never to destroy, just not by water. The rainbow was one kind of promise, a beautiful one, but it did not guarantee a life without hard stuff. "In this world, you will have trouble . . ." I'd heard Rev. Smithe say that back when Jed was very little.

"But fear not, for I have overcome the world," Alonso whispered. "That's the important part, Mavis. That's the crucial part."

I sat back and took a deep breath. He was right . . . that part of the verse, that's what I needed to remember.

As evening settled in, people began to make their way home across place and time. Alonso helped Mayuri send people back to their moments, and Mrs. Wilson with LaKeemba at her side offered the folks from now an invitation to return to the farm any time they needed a safe place to rest.

Most of us settled back in by the fire, but Mr. Wilson got into his truck. I thought he was probably going to get some hay and take it around the back of the pasture for the goats who had gathered there away from the crowd. But instead, he came back up with a cab full of food—Chinese, pizza, and Thai from this little hole-in-the-wall place that only locals knew had the best food around.

I grabbed a plate and jostled against Jed for a place in line just behind Sharon, who had never been shy about getting her share of food. It was a trait I admired greatly. I piled on egg rolls and pad Thai, and the mozzarella sticks called my name, too. I tried to save some space for the salad, but I figured I could come back for it later. A little delusion on a day like today was understandable.

Our conversation was quiet, subdued, but joyful. I remembered the day Jed's baseball team won the local championship when he was about eight. The boys were exuberant; the parents happy but also glad it was over for the year. Everyone was tired, so while we'd eaten pizza and the boys had done live-action replays of their favorite moments from the tournaments, all the adults had lain back against their blankets on the hillside behind home plate and stared at the sky. It felt like that now— joyful but tired.

After I had gotten my second brownie—and officially given up on the salad—I made my way over and sat next to Charlie. He'd taken a spot near the fire but a bit separate, and everyone had given him space, probably because none of us were sure what to say. His face was still, like he was thinking hard about something and needed some time to figure it out. I didn't want to leave him alone too long, though. I knew how it was to need space but also need people to come and check on me.

So I handed Charlie a brownie and sat down beside him on a wool blanket that we usually kept in the barn for the young goat kids. "You okay?" It was a dumb question, I knew. Of course, he wasn't okay, but I knew that if I asked him something more pointed, something more accurate, he might just bristle away. Better to stay casual.

He shrugged. "Maybe?"

I nodded. "Sounds about right. Want to talk about it?"

He shrugged again.

We sat there for a few minutes listening to the fire pop and our friends talk quietly.

Finally, he said, "Do you think I can visit him?"

"Your dad?" I looked at him.

He looked puzzled.

"Do you think you want to visit him?"

"I'm not sure. But it would help to know if I could if I wanted to. Don't want to get my hopes up if it's not possible, I figure." His voice was thin, and I could almost imagine him as a little boy, all that red hair and hope.

"I think that's a good question to ask LaKeemba. You know she'll tell you the truth." I looked over the fire and across the pasture to the farmyard across the road. "Was it hard to see him like that?"

"With The Shadow, you mean?" He followed my gaze and leaned back on his elbows. "Not really. I think, in a way, it might have made it easier to see him with that thing, The Shadow. At least then I could blame someone besides him."

An image of Charlie in the stocks on his farm, put there by his father to suffer, flashed behind my eyes. I'm not sure I could have survived that, that kind of betrayal. If I'd had Charlie's gift, I might have stopped time right before they put me in those things and then walked away, leaving everything on that farm trapped in that moment. But then, I hadn't lived through that, and the people I loved most hadn't ever treated me that horribly. They'd never forsaken me. That's how I thought of what Charlie's father had done.

"I guess I can see that. Better a monster than your dad."

He nodded. "But my dad is a monster, Mavis. Isn't he?" Tears were pooled in the bottom of Charlie's eyes.

It took everything I had not to reach over and hug him. I knew, though, that he didn't want a hug just now. He wanted another kind of reassurance. "I don't think any of us people are monsters, Charlie. We do horrible things because horrible things have been done to us. We make mistakes because we don't know better or because we're scared or because we're greedy. But we're not monsters. We're just people, and sometimes people do terrible things to each other."

I looked around at our friends gathered, and I thought of all the monstrous things that had been done to them and wondered about the things I didn't know about yet. "The monsters of this world, things like The Shadow, they just glom onto the awful feelings we have, our fear and our shame, our anger and our greed, and they amplify them. But those creatures, they don't make us monsters. We're still just people."

Charlie stared at me a minute and then looked away. "I think I'll go ask LaKeemba about visiting now." He stood up, and I laid back to look up at the stars. Then, Charlie bent down and kissed my cheek, like the grown man he was.

I rested there for a long time, watching the stars come out above me.

JEDIDIAH

When the farm was quiet, I began. Dad and Marcus had rigged up a series of posts, and the canvas was already up. Dad had offered to keep the fire going and to stay and keep me company, but I knew I needed to start this alone.

From the box of art supplies Mom had given me a few weeks back, I chose an orange pastel stick and began. His hair was the easy part. I could just picture Charlie's mop on his pillow in our room to get that, but when I started on Poke's face, I hesitated, not sure what to draw.

But then, I let go. Stopped thinking and let it come . . . and there, the boy Poke had been started to appear.

This little boy with his finger in a biscuit and molasses on the corners of his mouth, he was the first to be remembered. But not the last, never the last.

18

I woke up the next morning when a sunbeam found its way through my curtains and shone right on my face. I'd collapsed into bed without even bothering to change into pajamas. Apparently, I'd slept hard because when I rolled over, I felt my cheek land in a wet spot made from my drool. I couldn't even care. I was just so glad to be done with The Shadow.

When I had washed my face and slapped a baseball cap on over my wild hair, I stepped out onto my stoop and saw what I had hoped to see. Everything was back to normal: people were working in the garden by the farmhouse; children were chasing each other around the yurts; Mr. Wilson was peeling off flakes of hay for the goats. I stretched and strolled toward the farmhouse. A cup of coffee with Mrs. Wilson sounded just about perfect right then.

But as I headed across the pasture to the farmhouse, I saw something shimmering in the light. It was the most beautiful drawing I'd ever seen. Jed's art come to life. As far as I could see, there were faces, some smiling, some restful, but all at peace. At the end of the long field, Jed was still sketching.

Alonso came up beside me and squeezed my hand. "Something ain't it? I've been watching him all night. It's incredible."

"He's incredible," I said and squeezed Alonso's hand. "Come with me?"

"I'll be along shortly. Give you two a minute." He smiled at me, and I leaned down to kiss him.

I smiled as I headed toward my oldest friend.

When I reached the end of the field out by the road, I saw that Jed was actually drawing on what looked like a long sheet of fabric, not in the air like normal. "You got yourself some actual canvas this time, huh?" I said.

He looked at me out of the corner of his eye as he sketched the corner of a woman's full lips. "Didn't think we could get away with 'air art' when we're doing a showing."

"A showing? People are going to come see your work?"

Jed told me that he, his parents, and Sharon had been talking with a gallery owner, another magic person, for the past few months, strategizing how he could get his work out into the world. There had been plans, apparently, for him to do a solo show over the summer.

"They are. But it won't be a solo show, at least not really. The piece is called 'The Remembered.'" He paused in his drawing and turned toward me. Then, I saw the bottle tied to a leather cord, dangling below his collarbones. "I have a lot more people to draw, but others are helping, too."

As he returned to his sketch, he told me that with the help of Davesh, Mohindor, and other magic people around the world, artists were sketching, writing songs, sculpting, painting, and telling stories about the people from the bottle. "We're all going to keep creating until everyone is remembered."

I smiled. I liked that idea, but I couldn't help but worry, too. "Jed, you may never finish."

He nodded. "Probably not. But that's okay. This isn't bad for a life's work, right?"

I felt a hand slide against my waist. "I'd say not, Jedidiah Wilson. I'd say not," Alonso said. "You and I have work to do, too, you know?" He turned to me. "But first, I have a question."

Alonso and I got married a month later, right there on the farm with Jed's fabric mural as a backdrop for the ceremony. Our friends from all over the world and all along time joined us, and it was a wonderful party full of music and good food. I couldn't imagine anything better than having everyone I loved gathered in once place.

But soon after, Alonso and I got to work. Each day, we checked the map, and on the days she gave us a blue dot, we went carrying bags of costumes for the time and place. Sometimes we brought people back with us. Sometimes, we went and got the story before bringing back other friends to help with healing or mending or even a little time weaving. But we were the ambassadors, the ones went first to see. It was good work.

And Jed, well, Jed kept sketching. By the time he finished high school, he had a full scholarship for the Maryland Institute College of Art in Baltimore because of his work on The Remembered project, and that was just the beginning for him. He kept drawing those the bottle told him to draw, but he soon expanded his work to include the secrets he saw. He sketched those as tributes—sometimes with permission, sometimes with the person who owned them as a veiled figure—to the things we all keep hidden, the stories we don't tell.

Years later, when Alonso and I were old and gray, Jed came by to visit us after seeing his parents on a trip home from New York, where he was now working as an artist. Alonso and I had built our house just up the road from the Wilsons' farm.

Jed sat on our porch with a glass of sweet tea in his hand, and he said, "You two ready?"

I smiled at Alonso, and he nodded.

"Absolutely," I said. Then, I took the folded map out of the pocket of my sweater and leaned forward. "Molly, are you ready?

The twelve-year-old girl with white-blonde hair looked at her daddy and then at me. "I hope so," she said as she took the map from me and began to unfold it.

READ ABOUT THE FIRST TIME JED DISCOVERS HIS MAGIC

Get your FREE copy of *The Shadow. The Secret. The Shame*, the story of when Jed first discovered he could see people's secrets. Download it here - https://dl.bookfunnel.com/kx94oy4sin .

GHOSTS. SPELLS. PEOPLE WITH WILD ABILITIES

If these are your faves, then come on over and get all the magical realism books your TBR can handle. Weekly emails of magical realism and fantasy, especially for young adults and the young at heart. Plus, a few notices about my own books, too. Join my newsletter here:
andilit.com/magical-realism

ALSO BY ANDI CUMBO-FLOYD

ANDI CUMBO-FLOYD
CHARLOTTE AND THE TWELVE
The Steele Secrets Series Book 2

ANDI CUMBO-FLOYD
SILENCE AT THE LOCK
The Steele Secrets Series Book 3

ABOUT THE AUTHOR

Andi Cumbo-Floyd lives in Virginia's Southwestern Mountains with her young son, old hound, and a bully mix who has already eaten two couches. When she's not writing, she cross-stitches, watches YA fantasy shows, and grows massive quantities of cucumbers. Find out more about her at andilit.com.

9 781952 430459